D1253534

LESTER CAINE
PRIVATE EYE

MURDER ON PALM BEACH

Book One from Lester Caine Private Eye Series

(A stand alone book)

fred berri has won multiple 1st Prize Five Star prestigious International Literary Book Awards for his novels and children's books.

Readers' Favorite provides professional reviews for authors and has earned the respect of renowned publishers such as Random House, Simon & Schuster and Harper Collins. Readers' Favorite also tries to help those in need by donating books and income each year to *St. Jude Children's Research Hospital.*

Donate: https://www.stjude.org/donate/donate-to-st-jude.html?sc_dcm=58700007207518211&sc_cid=kwp&sc_cat=b&ds_rl=1285465&gclid=EAIaIQobChMIye32hL3q8QIVnGtvBB3aHwcTEAAYASABEgJv5fD_BwE&gclsrc=aw.ds

Firebird Book 5 Star Awards

Firebird Book Awards are sponsored by Speak Up Talk Radio that advocates *Enchanted Makeovers* which renovates and transforms long term shelters for women and children into places of peace and possibility. *Enchanted Makeovers* have impacted over 60, 000 people nationally. You can donate and help women and children. Visit to find out more & Donate:

https://enchantedmakeovers.org/programs-projects/

"Twist, turn and bend the truth.

Now it's fiction." ™

fredberri.com

Facebook:

https://www.facebook.com/fredberriwriter/

&

Instagram-LinkedIn-Twitter-Goodreads

Lester Caine-Private Eye-

Murder on Palm Beach

© 2021 frederic dalberri

LCCN 2022909299

Publisher frederic dalberri

Vero Beach, Florida

Lester Caine-Private Eye

Murder on Palm Beach

Book One from Lester Caine Private Eye Series

(A stand alone book)

All *rights reserved.* Reproducing or storing any portion of this book in a retrieval system, transmitted, or distributed in any form or by any means—electronic, mechanical, photocopy, recording, scanning, or other-- - without the prior written permission of the author is illegal and punishable by law except by a reviewer who may quote brief passages in a review printed in a newspaper, magazine or journal.

ISBN: 979-8-9855923-1-3 (Print)

ISBN: 979-8-9855923-2-0 (Ebook)

Reader Awareness

The story herein is for a mature audience containing adult material that includes coarse language, sexual content, and violence.

Dedication

To twenty six of my close friends who are always there at my beck and call. None of them have ever denied or failed me when I call on them-Ever!

I will introduce them to you by name on the following pages.

***

NOTE FROM THE AUTHOR

This story is fictional. Any names, characters, places, or situations are purely coincidental and are a "fougasse[1]" Any similarity to real persons, living or dead is coincidental and not intended by the author, with the exception of historical events, historical dates, or any actual locations, and facts.

---

[1] Fougasse /fuːˈgɑːs/ is a term used for "fake" or not real. The word originated back in the seventeenth century to describe a fake rock that was filled with explosives during wars. Soldiers would step on these fake rocks, exploding the bomb and causing serious injury or death. So the rock being fake or not real was termed a *fougasse*. This novel is a fougasse.

My Twenty-Six Close Friends By Name:

A B C D E F G H I J K L M N O P Q R S T U V W X Y
Z

All my novels and children's books I write with the use

of only twenty-six letters. Thank you, my friends.

"Cogito, ergo sum"

"I think, therefore I am"

René Descartes (1596 – 1650)

TABLE OF CONTENTS

FOREWORDS

---

fred berri's books take me right back to those great mystery / detective reads I loved growing up set in the 40s with no techies to break the case. Just old-fashioned gum shoe. Murder On Palm Beach takes me to a place I love and to read about–and a fearless detective that I just wish I could meet."

Jennifer Munro
National Speaker and President, Eaglevision Performance Solutions, Inc.
Eaglevisonteam.com
Amazon Best Selling Author

"Get ready for another power-packed fred berri thriller/mystery; Lester Caine, Private Eye. This is another can't-put-it-down session in your house. When I want thriller action with a bite, I pick up one of my fred Berri books. This is another you will love. "

Larry David Allman
Lawyer and former International Diplomat
Amazon Best-Selling Author

"Wow, Fred Berri has done it again! If you like a true, down-to-earth, no-nonsense private detective who can bend and twist the rules to get the job done, then Lester Caine is your man. I couldn't put the book down!"

Celia Milano

Trustee for The Sicilian Project
Platinum Member of Laura Riding Jackson Foundation dedicated to writers
Amazon Best Selling author

"Having read other mystery books by Fred Berri, this is another of his latest that includes intrigue, humor and a healthy dose of spice".

Ellen Gillette / Emily Sharpe
Amazon Best Selling Authors

Murder among the Palm Beach elite; a judge killed in his home. The Palm Beach Police summon retired New York detective Lester Caine.

fred berri turns the clock back to an era of development, opportunity, mercenaries, and mobsters in Miami and Palm Beach. *Lester Caine Private Eye, Murder on Palm Beach* shows Florida's past through the eyes of cops, priests, showgirls, attorneys, and more. Readers of detective fiction will enjoy the ride in Lester's 1948 Series 62 Horizon Blue Caddy convertible.

jc konitz, Editor
Five Star Readers Favorite Author
Becoming Kate, a novel of second chances
Herald the Christmas Dachshund

PROLOGUE

L ester Caine was a former cop with a blemished file that could have tarnished his reputation and retirement, but Lester always landed on his feet.

Lester never looked back at what he left behind in New York City. The flickering neon lights of the all-night diners that catered to cops, hookers, Broadway actors or any drunk that stumbled into *Chuck Full of Nuts* for a cup of coffee or the smell of knishes emanating from the open sidewalk windows of *Nedick's* restaurant.

He admitted, however, he missed the hookers he affectionately called his snitches and his frequent haunts of The Savoy and Lenox Lounge Jazz clubs, where he could express himself artistically playing some serious notes on his trumpet with the likes of jazz artist, Billy Holiday. He could have played as he dreamed with the famous musicians, but his father's death held him to the fire of getting the bad guys off the streets.

New York City was a smorgasbord of evil filled with huge concrete and steel towers of Babel that dwarfed Don Quixote's windmills. He loved what he traded: the cold, snowy bleak winters for sweltering dog day summers with no air conditioning; the foul smell of urine in the subway stations for golden sand, women

4

sunning on loungers, soft tropical breezes, palm trees, and the socialites of Palm Beach. His pension accorded him the privilege of driving those Cadillac convertibles that always turned the ladies' heads.

Lester chose West Palm Beach for two reasons. His mother moved to Lake Worth, close and yet far enough to sustain their strained relationship. The other was his foresight.

Henry Flagler planned West Palm Beach to be a residential community for employees of his hotels. It was well planned, with palm-lined streets, a teeming waterfront and upscale neighborhoods. When the sun set, a variety of restaurants served epicurean tastes and made dining by candlelight a delight.

Lester, like Henry Flagler, was a visionary. He knew that residents and business owners would need his specialty—investigating crimes, fraud, and recovery of stolen art and jewels. With crime came lawyers, bail bondsmen and district attorneys, all in need of private investigators.

Lester wore his gun on his left hip, often referred to by his cohorts in blue as *cowboy style*. He angled it with a 20-degree forward slant holster, drawing with his right hand. He was a real cop, a cop's cop. Well, he had been at one time anyway, a former Lieutenant Detective, hard-boiled right out of New York City–the kind they don't make anymore–now retired.

He faced off in two shoot-outs during his twenty-five-year career on the force.

Hank Bauman had an arrest warrant for murder. Lester was in charge of the raid on the house where Hank was hiding out in Riverdale, a pleasant neighborhood of well-kept homes along the Hudson River, just north of Manhattan. As protocol, the Bronx detectives and sharpshooters joined the scene. No one knew if Hank was alone or if there were hostages. The tip came from one of Lester's snitches, a hooker Hank regularly used. The painted ladies of the night knew where their bread was buttered and it was not from their Johns or their clients. It was quid pro quo, this for that, and Lester knew how to use it.

The police secured the perimeter of the two-story house. Lester got the bull-horn: "Hank, this is your friend, Lieutenant Caine. Look out the window. There's no getting out of this one, Hank."

Lester saw the curtain twitch. "C'mon, Hank. You don't want to do this. I can help you. Come out, Hank."

Hank smashed the glass window, shards falling on the lawn, sparkling in the police floodlights, putting the snipers on edge, and raising their weapons.

"Hank, don't be stupid. I know you see what's out here waiting for you. Don't do this. Come out peacefully. I will help you. I promise." Lester continued, trying to get Hank engaged, knowing there was no way in Hell he was going to get Hank out of this.

"I have hostages," Hank yelled out through the jagged edge of the window.

"No, you don't, Hank. There's no one in there with you, so come out."

"NO!"

Hank fired one round through the open window. The bullet ricocheted off one of the police cars.

"Hold your fire!" Lester yelled, his voice echoing through the bull horn.

"You should not have done that," Lester called out, approaching the front door. "Hank, you're not cooperating."

Lester saw the door open slowly. No one spoke. "Hank, look at me." Lester had taken his suit jacket and holster off, placing them on the hood of the police car. "I'm unarmed," raising his hands above his head, he stepped forward slowly.

"I've never seen anything like this," one sniper said. "This bastard must have brass balls."

"Yeah. They say he clicks when he walks," his partner replied.

"Stop right there. Turn around slow, all the way around," Hank demanded to reassure himself Lester was not hiding any weapons.

Lester followed Hank's instructions, turning in a circle, hands in the air, freeing his tucked in shirt to reveal a glimpse of bare chest and back.

"Okay, take one step at a time and come in or I'll kill my guests here."

Lester took a big chance calling Hank's bluff, hoping there were no hostages. He entered through the door, following procedure just as his rookie training had taught him, tilting his head to be sure Hank was not waiting behind the door.

"Over here, Lieutenant," Hank called to Lester.

"*Shit!*" Lester mumbled, seeing Hank point his gun at the two hookers sitting on the couch.

One woman whispered through her sobs, "Lester, I did not sign up for this."

"Ha, ha, Lieutenant. Too bad it's not April fool. I told you I had hostages. They're your informants. Stupid bitches."

The young women were crying. Their mascara ran down their faces, giving the illusion of masquerading as witches on Halloween. This seemed to excite Hank. He puffed his chest and looked at them with a superior sneer. Then, he turned to Lester. "Get on your knees," Hank said. Lester complied.

"Put the gun down and let me walk you out of here. You see what's outside. You have me. Let them go," Lester said.

"Like hell. They're coming with me. One of these bitches is why you're here," Hank said as he cocked the hammer on his revolver.

Lester's stint as firearms instructor one summer during his tenure on the force identified what Hank held in his hand—a Colt single-action .45 caliber army six-shooter revolver with a five and a half inch barrel. He knew the collateral damage this beast of a gun could do. Hank only needed to fire two rounds–one to each of the hookers.

Lester knew a shooter could do it if he was fast enough. Hank must cock the hammer back–releasing it to fire the bullet and repeat it to get both women. He pictured this in his mind's eye, seeing the cylinder rotate to the right with six rounds. Lester could not hesitate. On his knees, he could grab the revolver strapped to his ankle for easy carrying—a Smith and Wesson .38 snub-nose with a two-inch barrel. A versatile revolver, many cops carried it for a back-up piece either as a double action–not having to cock the hammer, or use it as a single action cocking the hammer back. He only needed to fire one round off to stop Hank.

BLAM! The blast was deafening, making your ears ring. One hooker screamed, a shrill assault on his ears. Hank's brain splattered blood, gray matter, tissue, and bone fragments everywhere—the curtains, furniture and the two young women who shook uncontrollably. The stink of body fluids between Hank and the women was almost unbearable. Lester swallowed hard, forcing a lump of bile down his throat.

The police snipers stormed the house like wild buffalos in a stampede, stomping into every room yelling: "CLEAR."

Hank lay slumped across the coffee table, a hole in his head, eyes wide open,—dead.

Years later...

Lester came face to face with Ray *Squeaky* McMillan, a wanted murderer.

This was the second time Lester fired his weapon in the twenty-five years in the line of duty. His ricochet bullet hit *Squeaky* in the right eye, making him now half blind. Squeaky never lost his sense of humor, often saying that the man with one eye in the Land of the Blind is King.

Squeaky got his name from the high-pitched whistling sound he made when he sneezed. *Squeaky* was on Death Row, waiting for his eventual destination for killing his wife and mother-in-law. He claimed his innocence–self-defense, although between the two women there were one hundred and five stab wounds.

Every single bullet fired by a police officer has to be accounted for, and they must pay a visit to the department's psychiatrist. The Departmental Review Board justified both of Caine's shootings. There was never a Grand Jury.

Lester, in his wildest dreams, could have never imagined he would run into someone years later from his New York City days, over a thousand miles away from his past. Someone fondly known as one of his snitches and needing his help.

Lester didn't think of turning his back on someone asking for his help, no matter how long it had been, where they've been, or where they were now. If they needed his help, Lester gave them his full attention, but knowing his reputation, they were going to pay and pay big time for Lester Caine.

There was, however, something Lester could not escape. The continuous contentious obligations he knew he had. He could not turn his back on his mother, Pamela, who lived in Lake Worth for the past few years, getting out of the Bronx to enjoy whatever time she had left in her corner of paradise on God's good earth, as she would say.

It was a continuous revolving conversation between mother and son as opposing attorneys in a courtroom. Yet, Lester would never shirk his obligations.

CHAPTER I

West Palm Beach, Florida,

1948

W ord spread upon Lester's arrival after retiring his NYC Detective's shield. He was back in the cop business–the business of private investigations. Lester didn't have to answer to anybody any longer, just himself and the monthly bills that came in like clockwork. His office was on Clematis Street with gold leaf lettering painted on an opaque pane of glass covering the top half of the door, making it official.

Lester Caine

Private Investigations

The pre-war office building was in downtown West Palm Beach, Florida, in reach of the courthouse, attorneys, and bail bondsman. Lester knew his way around the block. His reputation had grown since his landing in Palm Beach two years ago. He had a lot of testosterone and was too young to escort little old ladies across the street or take up fishing. Besides, he loved the law and knew how to skirt around *things* to be in his favor. Now Lester was a private eye with a license to carry his own piece, not one issued by the NYPD.

Lester dressed impeccably—a freshly pressed and tailored Brooks Brothers suit, white shirt, silk tie, and Allen-Edmond shoes. If the suit and shoes were good enough for US Naval Officers and US Presidents to wear, then they had to be good enough for him.

He stood six feet in his stocking feet with a chiseled jaw displaying a proud cleft chin and compelling, piercing hazel eyes, immediately capturing the women. Lester had become somewhat of a celebrity with the ladies over the years. He became known as the romance novel cover cop. Divorced twice with no kids and no alimony to contend with, he liked his freedom, women, Jim Beam Bourbon and his Cadillac.

Now he was free to pursue his methods, not conforming to what he viewed as the stifling book of rules and regs. He used to do that. Cops have to follow procedure. Now he got information out of someone by sticking the barrel of his gun to their head, and cocking the hammer back.

He didn't have to go easy. Once he saw beads of sweat on their foreheads, he knew he had an informer exactly where he wanted–in the hot seat that usually produced the answers he was looking for. Lester could find the dirt on people, and he found it his way. The attorneys, bail bondsmen, and cops knew Lester would get any information or find whoever they needed for their client or the cases they were working. He was foremost on their list to hire.

CHAPTER 2

L ouise, Caine's secretary, always arrived early, doing things in an organized manner. First, she would go through the mail that fell through the slot in the door from the mailman's delivery. Next, she would call the answering service to collect all Lester's messages. What didn't wind up in the trash basket was on Caine's desk.

The office was simple and functional, since Lester didn't hang around much. He was a mover and a shaker. When you opened the door, a musty smell assailed your nostrils.

Louise would greet those entering her space with a smile and her southern hospitable manner. "Would you like coffee and a donut while you wait?"

Lester, moved by her charm and her competent manner, hired her on the spot, not bothering to interview anyone else. And she had been with him from day one. Louise grew up in Florida and was well versed and worldly wise with what life offered. She grew up fast, having to care for two younger sisters. Her demeanor was that of an aging debutant, but her bite was pure pit-bull. Louise had a license to carry, and that she did—a .38 caliber. Lester himself carried the same. He said; 'His revolver was like a woman who would never jam on you when you're relying on her.'

Louise's sashay not only turned every man's head conspicuously, but it was one that should be against the law. She knew how to use it and use it well. She did what she needed to do to survive caring for her sisters. Her father worked the fields as a day worker when he was sober. Her mother packed up and left for California with a man she met, a stranger, never to see her again. Through it all, Louise was a charmer.

Her desk and large waiting area were all in one. Two leather chairs, couch, and file cabinets. On the walls hung pictures of Lester in his NYPD uniform with Mayors, Governors, and Police Chiefs with his awards and police ribbons.

Lester's door separated their domains with just one word in gold leaf:

PRIVATE

Lester's office also had two chairs with two adjoining rooms. One housed couch and coffee table. The other, just storage. Behind his desk hung the American Flag, framed under glass with his Purple Heart. He considered it his *Red Badge of Courage.* Since he spilled his blood on Dominican Republic soil when his Naval Unit's amphibious vehicle landed to take control and occupy the Dominican Republic. Lester's unit engaged in what was part of the Banana Wars—a series of military action conflicts, comprising occupation, police action and intervention by the United States—all key positions in the government and control of the army and police. This was only one of the many interventions in Latin America by the US military force. A major engagement occurred that the Dominicans had fortified and long thought of being invulnerable. Navy troops launched a bayonet charge on the defenders' first line of defense toward the hostile forces. Here is where Lester's blood lay.

Louise heard the keys jingle in the door, calling out; "It's open, Lester."

"Good morning, Louise... Ah!" Lester let out a sigh, taking in the aroma of fresh coffee and donuts. It was always a welcome start of his day, not knowing what the rest might bring.

Louise preferred the scent of Lester's *Old Taylor of Bond Street cologne* he imported from London. Its distinctive sandalwood fragrance always created a warm, deep fuzzy feeling in her, encouraging her libido. Lester interrupted her thoughts.

"There's money in the cash box. Be sure to take some for the donuts. Are there—"

"On your desk, Lester. Mail to the right and messages to the left," Louise interrupted. "There's an important one on top from Ron Walker of the Palm Beach Police."

"Hmm. From the police?" he mumbled.

"He said he needs you before you sit down, pronto."

The Palm Beach Police welcomed Lester, knew he could do whatever he chose to get results, what they couldn't get away with. The Police had to answer to every one of their actions, most times, anyway.

"Palm Beach Police, Homicide. Lieutenant Walker."
He answered his desk phone.

"It's Lester Caine, Ron."

"Caine, I need you right away. Don't even hang up
your hat."

Lester smiled, thinking; *I stopped wearing a dress
hat. There's a Panama on the front seat of my Caddy I
wear for the ladies now and then.*

"I'm on my way to a crime scene. I'm gonna need you
on this one."

Ron knew one thing for sure—he didn't want to know
Lester's methods of getting to the bottom of things. That
was confidential. In the private cop business, a free-
lancer didn't explain his methods.

Ronald Walker was a man of few words... mostly, and
abided by the books. He came to realize sometimes
there were gray areas that made law enforcement turn
its head in order to solve a crime. The good guys win
and the bad guys lose.

Ron came to Florida with his parents after they lost
their farm. The depression started in the Midwest long
before the Wall Street Crash of 1929. Drought hit the
Great Plains during the Great Depression.

A severe drought turned the soil to dust on the
Walker Farm. Ron's father packed up the family and
wrangled his way to manage a Florida orange grove,
supplying and shipping oranges throughout the
country.

The manager's compensation included free housing for the family with an on-site cottage. Ron and his mother ran the small roadside retail store. That was part and parcel of the deal. The police and detectives would stop for their weekly gift basket containing oranges and freshly squeezed bottled orange juice.

The story Ron heard intrigued him. Two teenage girls were raped and murdered; their nude bodies dumped in the canal in Okeechobee. Every story thereafter further moved him. He decided to be a detective. Every chance he got, he took money from his tip jar and bought *True Detective Magazine* with its complete and detailed stories and real crime scene photos.

Lester took the stairs, a faster way down than the clunky elevator, to achieve what Lieutenant Walker asked of him... get there yesterday.

CHAPTER 3

Palm Beach, Florida.

L ester pulled into the circular driveway. Yellow crime scene tape already strewn all around the front yard kept the neighbors and reporters from crossing. The uniforms were knocking on doors and questioning neighbors already gathered out front.

"Let 'em through," Lieutenant Walker shouted from the open front door.

One uniformed officer raised the tape for Lester after he flashed his credentials, ignoring the reporters that beat him there. Crime reporters picked up the news from their police scanners. They yelled his name with questions, hoping he'd turn for a photo shot and maybe this was the day he would answer them.

"Lester, what can you tell us?"

"C'mon, Lester, give us something we can go on."

"Caine, just this one time, anything."

"Not today, fellas," was Lester's standard pitch, not breaking his stride.

"Jesus H Christ, it's already a circus out there," Walker mumbled.

Lester Caine stood in the living room of 1868 Wilshire Court, the lavish home of the Honorable Desmond Vanderbilt and his wife, Lorraine. He could not miss the panoramic views of the Atlantic Ocean through the open French doors that overlooked the pool as soon as he stepped foot inside.

It was a magazine layout straight out of House and Garden that smacked him square in the face. The Palm Beach Police were like ants scurrying from here to there.

"Caine, you've got to see this. You will not believe it," Walker said, introducing Lester to the crime scene. Walker's men were milling around, searching each room, opening drawers and closets, hunting for clues. The crime scene techs were swirling their brushes, spreading the resin, black ferric oxide and lampblack powder while the flash and click from another cop's camera took photos.

I bet they won't find any prints, but they have to do their job. Why was His Honor lying dead in his own living room? Lester thought, uneasy from the moment he read the room as a seasoned detective, looking for what wasn't there.

Judge Desmond Vanderbilt never imagined his life would end in murder. His honor was a stout man, bold, strong-minded and vigorous. Vanderbilt, although raised on a farm, oozed city slicker. He dressed handsomely, wearing his trademark bow ties with wide suspenders that buttoned fashionably to his pants to help keep them up from his slightly protruding beer belly. He loved his imported cigars and the law. Desmond embellished the law's details and features, following it to a tee to those that stood before him in his courtroom.

The lectures His Honor gave were interesting and entertaining, with extra details that eased the actual sentence itself that he imposed when his gavel struck the sounding block. That sound officially entered the prisoner's sentence to the court record, rendering it final. He executed harsh sentences prescribed by law with such grace that condemned prisoners would thank him.

Lester sat many times in his courtroom as His Honor skillfully promulgated sentences on those miscreants that Lester and the Police brought to justice.

Now Judge Desmond Vanderbilt lay on the living room carpet, staining the imported Persian rug, crimson red, his head oozing blood from a gun-shot wound.

The gun was in full view. Was it someone else imposing a death sentence and dropping the gavel on the judge? Was it murder, an accident or self-inflicted, committing suicide?

Judge Desmond Vanderbilt was minutes away from being sworn into the Florida Supreme Court chosen by direct election of the people. He met the required criteria: a Florida resident and voter, a member of the Florida Bar for over ten years, and under the age of seventy-five. His Honor, forty-nine years old, lay in the *dead man's fall,* where in a crazy phenomenon, the ankles cross as a spinal reflex when the victim is brain dead. *He had a most sought after brilliant legal mind in the state and the country. Now, this brilliant mind is gone*

Lester's thoughts raced. *Suicide makes little sense. Suicide is permanence to a temporary situation. His career was on a political fast track, starting with a Judgeship to the Florida Supreme Court. There is no way he did himself in.*

Little did Palm Beach Police Lieutenant Ron Walker know that he and the Judge had something in common. They were both raised on a farm. What they didn't have in common came with the dark side of Desmond Vanderbilt.

"You know she asked for you, Caine." Walker pointed to the formal dining room. "She didn't want to talk with anyone until you arrived. She's gonna need an attorney. I'm allowing this because of who he was—a personal favor from me and from him," nodding his head toward the Honorable Desmond Vanderbilt's body, a body that soon would have been a member of Florida's Supreme Court.

"Lieutenant, the Coroner is here," muttered one cop.

"Show him where the body is. It's show time, Caine. She's waiting for you. Don't fuck this up on me."

CHAPTER 4

Mrs. Vanderbilt had no expression. She only moved to drag on her Pall Mall cigarette. She sipped her vodka in between drags. Lester noticed the lipstick-stained butts that filled the ashtray. *Were they from yesterday? Are they from today? How long has she been sitting here smoking and drinking?* Her demeanor didn't win her points. Walker was right.

From the looks of things, Lorraine was going to need a top-notch defense attorney, one like Desmond was a long time ago. He had earned his wealth defending criminals.

Mrs. Vanderbilt knew Lester's reputation. They both originated from the streets–a former entertainer and a hard-boiled cop that would not stand for any bullshit, who made sure he righted the wrong. This was some big wrong for sure, and Mrs. Vanderbilt wanted it made right. No mistakes or frame-ups.

She had bounced around from here and there with no proper direction–a father who had run out on her and his wife, Lorraine's mother, and was footloose and fancy free.

Lorraine climbed up from entertained to running a prominent gentleman's steak house owned by the mob. She met Desmond there. Years earlier, he was a regular when he and his partners ran a defense attorney's law firm in Miami. Their clients were high-powered thugs. Lightning hit Desmond Vanderbilt when he first saw Lorraine on stage. Gentlemen wore the standard suit jacket and tie. The ladies wore dresses or business pantsuits contrasting with the lady servers and stage entertainers who were topless. Scanty G-strings and pasties covered their assets as required by law.

Lorraine was still a looker. She was turning fifty, even with beginning crow's feet wrinkles etched in the corner of her eyes that she couldn't hide with the powdered hydrating foundation she used. They appeared more pronounced than the other few lines appearing on her face. In Lester's opinion, these showed her knowledge gained through years of living. Her body still held its shape; her dancer's long legs still youthful. Her relatively smooth skin contrasted sharply with her dark ginger auburn hair, like the burned orange sunset over Siesta Key. Lester recalled *she was a real doll in her day*. Rumor has it she ran one of Chicago's finest brothels before moving to New York.

"Lorraine, we need to talk."

"I'm glad you came, Lester. I need your help," she said, sincerely asking as a friend.

"Excuse us boys," Lester gestured to the uniformed cops standing guard to leave the room.

"It's been a long time, Lester. Let me pour you a drink. Bourbon, if I...?"

Lester lit up a smoke, tapping it first on his lighter—a habit to pack the tobacco tighter.

"Yeah, it has been a long time. And I'll take that drink. I don't miss the New York rat race. Twenty-five years on the force and New York wore on me. I'm glad I'm here. Tell me something that I can use," Lester said, wanting to hear her innocence, ready to jot some notes.

"I saw you always as a straight shooter, even the times you busted me when you were a street cop. You never treated me, well, you know. You always treated me with respect. Let me keep my dignity. There are no blank pages with you, Lester. Too bad you married. I could have fallen for you."

Lester let out a guttural, low laugh. "That ship sailed the harbor two times. Look around, honey. I'd say it worked out for you."

"Looks can deceive," she said with a sigh.

"Go ahead, I'm all ears. You have my full attention—for old times' sake. First, let me ask—did you kill Desmond?"

Lorraine knew that question would come up eventually and was glad it was sooner coming from Lester.

Being the seasoned cop that he was, Lester's gut told him the moment he viewed the room where Desmond's body lay that it was too sterile, too calculated. Like an operating room. Their housekeeper kept the place pristine, but this was a different clean. Everything seemed in its place, like the surgical instruments lined up at attention, ready to jump at the doctor's command. Everything in its proper place, even the patient on the operating table. So, too, with Desmond. He lay there as expected a dead man should, the gun in its proper place next to him, just like the surgeon's tools next to him.

CHAPTER 5

Twenty Years earlier...

1928

Miami Beach was in its infancy, about to experience growing pains. This was a city ready for metamorphosis, transforming from an unspoiled native habitat to a magic city with many people who would profit as it grew. Sandpits, mangroves, marshlands, and mosquitoes originally comprised the city, the only place in Florida where you could find both alligators and crocodiles. It all had to go.

The founders and industry leaders knew this Florida city could attract thousands by turning it into a cash-making machine, even with the economic bubble that burst in 1926. Money and credit ran out, and banks and investors abruptly stopped trusting the *paper* millionaires. Severe hurricanes swept through the state. By the time the Great Depression began in the rest of the nation in 1929, Floridians were already accustomed to economic hardship. The founding fathers had the foresight to see that Miami would recover. So did Desmond Vanderbilt. Airlines and railroads expanded their routes to Florida and a coalition of judges, lawyers, politicians, journalists, brewers and hoteliers organized to repeal the ban on alcohol and subsequently joined in the national campaign to repeal the Eighteenth Amendment. In addition, they wanted to legalize gambling. Desmond and his partners were part of that coalition.

None of the economic strife throughout the United States affected bootlegging, gambling or prostitution, and they were on the way to Miami.

Miami soon became host to notorious characters, including the most infamous gangster, Al Capone. Capone arrived in Miami in 1926, making this his getaway from cold Chicago winters and assassination attempts. This beautiful seaside community became a haven for real estate developers, politicians, and the mob, which brought the fallout of crime—lawlessness and corruption. Cuba was only ninety miles offshore and a haven for the mob.

Capone was arrested several times in Miami and jailed once. Constant surveillance or prison did not drive him out. Released from prison two months early for good behavior, Capone returned to Miami.

Miami wanted money and growth minus Big Al. One thing was for sure, no matter what city officials did, they could not ward off the trail of blood that trailed behind Capone. The mob poured in money, women, and booze. The gangster population increased, and hotels, nightclubs and beach resorts flourished.

Big Al pawned himself off as a secondhand furniture dealer, but Miami Beach knew Capone was no legitimate businessman regardless of his outward appearance of respectability. He was known for his discipline and was labeled the "gentleman gangster." Miami shuddered upon his arrival. Residents feared Capone's presence would convince the country that Miami Beach was no longer the good clean fun it had been in 1920.

Newspapers and city officials accused Capone of bringing gambling to the city; but with or without him, South Florida was a hotbed of illegal gambling, prostitution, corruption, and rum-running. City officials had looked the other way. The *Miami News* led the campaign to drive Capone out, but he wouldn't budge. In fact, he made Miami Beach his home, choosing Clarence Busch's Palm Island estate as his permanent residence.

Desmond Vanderbilt saw the vision of Miami's future and latched onto its shirt tails just like he learned in his youth from the book of Zechariah in the *Old Testament.* 'They shall take hold of the skirt of the Jew, saying, we will go with you, for we have heard God is with you.'

Not that Desmond was religious by all means or would humble himself to overcome his hubris toward a God, accepting that a benevolent, merciful God would allow such suffering and atrocities that continued in the world. He saw and understood a good thing when he saw it and took advantage like the Israelites had...to simply take hold of a good thing, even though his heritage was Dutch Catholic.

As a young attorney, just starting out in his chosen profession, he knew he didn't want to be a farmer in the Great Plains like his family. To their chagrin, farming became an arduous, grueling life of despair. The harsh climate with tornadoes, blizzards, drought, hail, floods, and grasshoppers that many farmers viewed as equal to plagues of biblical proportions soon besieged them. Climate and nature ultimately ruined crops and ruined them financially.

He studied how farmers were pushed from their land by greedy bankers who foreclosed on hard working folks unable to pay their loans. The farmers fell on hard times, but these bankers cared more for a fly that landed on cow shit! Desmond felt these people needed someone to stick up for them. They suffered from conditions out of their control, and the promise in the birth of a new nation died in the lives of many.

People charged with a crime they may or may not have committed affected Desmond in the same way. They were bamboozled like the Great Plains farmers. Desmond would not let that happen. He became a defense attorney at twenty-eight. He partnered with two of his law school chums, Libby St. James and Henry Harper. Both came from money and important connections. Besides, Desmond knew he would get some business from Big Al, whether for him or his henchmen. Someone in Capone's entourage would need a top-notch defense attorney sooner or later.

Henry Harper, nicknamed "H-2" has roots in early Americana where the Harpers settled along the eastern shore of Savannah, Georgia, around the time of the American Revolution.

The long established Harper name rose to prominence through land and investments. They were prominent ship owners, running cargo to trade with

South America. The Harper's wealth from the shipping industry to this day helped establish H-2's law practice.

Libby St. James's family arrived in the central district in the City of Westminster, London, after the Norman Conquest of 1066, established as one of the most aristocratic residential areas in Britain. The chatter through the years was that the St. James's name surfaced in Cape Town, South Africa, when the Cape was still a colony of the British Empire, bestowing wealth and world connections on the family.

Almost three years to the day after the splashdown of Al Capone in the heart of Miami Beach the three friends established their law firm, soon becoming the most sought after by the likes of characters right out of Damon Runyon's[2] story book. Their billboards read:

Vanderbilt, Harper & St. James

Attorneys for the Defense and Devil's Advocate

Miami became the focus of many men who desired wealth and glamor, rising from the swamp it once was to a beautiful rose. However, this rose had thorns that waited to bleed many men of life, liberty, and their pursuit of happiness.

---

2. Damon Runyon was an American Journalist and writer known for his seedy characters of gamblers, race-track bookies, gangsters and other habitués of the street.

CHAPTER 6

D esmond Vanderbilt got a free ride with a full scholarship at Stanford Law School. Unlike his partners, Libby and H-2, whose families could pave the way for them, Desmond's education wasn't free. He worked hard and long hours, both studying and working a job to help his family financially and save some money while away at law school.

During summers, Desmond clerked for two District Court Judges—Sanford Law Alumni, who favored him over the other clerks.

His Honor Dasby Warner's family originated in France and settled in New Orleans. He loved the law like any lawyer ought to, but didn't like the injustices he witnessed growing up against people of color and decided at an early age to speak up about what was right and what was wrong. The judge had seen a lot of wrong in the deep South, including fixed court trials for those defendants and plaintiffs favored by the judges and the law. Judge Warner came to despise what he witnessed.

And there was His Honor Harris Bleakly. The Harris name was his mother's maiden name. The Bleakleys traced their lineage back to the Anglo-Saxon Tribes of Britain. The shores of the New World welcomed many oppressed English families that lacked opportunity in their homeland. Thousands left at great expense. Those that survived were rewarded with enormous opportunities to change their lives. The English settlers made significant contributions to the colonies that eventually became the United States. The Bleakleys settled in Virginia.

The Honorable Harris Bleakly continued the family tradition of contributing significantly to society as a District Court Judge.

Dasby and Harris admired Desmond and often said; *'What's there not to like about him?'* He worked harder and longer than the other law clerks, accomplishing more than the judges asked of him. He also had a contact that supplied him with fresh Fonseca Cuban cigars known for their detail— dressed in silk tissue paper, a mild smoke, and fragrant aroma. And, let's not forget, the supply of Jack Daniel's Tennessee Whiskey Desmond received for giving legal advice to simple legal queries like real estate ownership, liens, debts owed, or arrests for disorderly conduct. Not yet a "practicing" attorney, he advised those who could not afford a lawyer. Many evenings turned into advanced secondary schooling for Desmond with Dasby, Harris, Fonseca, and Jack Daniels.

Desmond took a position as a junior attorney with a respected law firm in Miami, Florida, upon the recommendations and connections of Dasby Warner and Harris Bleakly. Desmond did not waver or jump at every opportunity put before him. He set his goal to develop into one of Miami's best defense attorneys, a mover and shaker for what he felt would be all good things, not yet having had his naivete pushed aside. Day by day, week by week, month by month, and year by year, Desmond did not relent by making friends, contacts, and plea deals. Each decision furthered his budding career, making a name for himself as one of the most sought-after defense attorneys.

CHAPTER 7

Opening the plush new law offices of *Vanderbilt, Harper & St. James* at 73 West Flagler Street in the newly constructed Dade County Court House was a wise move.

The courthouse had twenty-eight floors and was constructed at a cost of $4,000,000 the previous year. This area was the central business district most frequently used to shop, work and bank. It also housed Bail Bondsmen, the US Post Office, restaurants, the pink and blue painted façade advertising the famed Burdines Department Store on East Flagler and other merchants

Desmond, Libby and H-2 were an instant success. Desmond and H-2 wore tailored suits while Libby wore worsted wool tweed skirts and jackets. They were good looking, savvy to the ways of the world and highly educated in the law that each of them held dear to their hearts. They worked long and hard to achieve that sheepskin that hung on the walls of their offices.

Monday mornings rolled in fast after the weekend cocktail and celebratory parties that were common in Miami. The office hummed with the sound of fresh coffee percolating, releasing the aroma and wafting throughout, like a woman ready to receive her lover.

Two well-groomed men walked in, seeking an attorney. The receptionist buzzed Desmond.

"Mr. Vanderbilt, there are two gentlemen here, new clients. You are the only one without morning appointments." She whispered, *"They're priests."*

"Send them in, Rhonda." Desmond stood, welcomed them, and introduced himself, as did the priests.

"Mr. Vanderbilt, I'm Monsignor O'Malley." Turning, he looked down his nose. "This is Father Fairchild." Desmond offered coffee and sat back to listen.

"Father Fairchild has committed a terrible act in the eyes of our Lord and Savior. Mr. Vanderbilt, you may know how we regard sins in the Catholic Church."

"It's been a long time. However, before you continue, Monsignor, this sounds like confession is in order with an act of contrition. That's the essence of a sacrament and is an inscrutable process. I am not in the Holy Ghost business."

"Mr. Vanderbilt, this is far greater than a mere confession. A venial sin only weakens the soul with sickness but doesn't kill the grace within, like minor infections in the body. Then there are *mortal* sins that are not done accidentally," the Monsignor said.

"The person who commits a mortal sin is one who knows their sin is wrong, but deliberately commits the sin anyway. Many *venial* sins become easier to commit over and over, thus becoming the gateway to the more serious one–the *mortal* sin. This sin is truly a rejection of God's law and love and requires repentance. The punishment is great or not, depending on the sinner's remorse. Father Fairchild has committed the most heinous *mortal* sin of all."

"Monsignor," Desmond stood, holding his hand out. "Stop right here! As an officer of the court, I cannot hear about a crime without first establishing client–attorney relationship. You must sign an Attorney–Client Representation Agreement. Otherwise, I have to report the crime to the authorities."

"Mr. Vanderbilt, your firm has represented some unsavory characters that entered the Den of Iniquity and walked out unscathed. As Monsignor, I have the privilege of representing the Church through the Archdiocese. Where do I sign?"

"Now, Monsignor, I must hear this from Father Fairchild," Desmond said, following the formalities. "So, I must ask you to sit quietly while my secretary takes notes."

"Rhonda," he said over the office intercom, "come in with your steno pad. Father Fairchild, let's begin at the beginning of the act Monsignor O'Malley is referring to as your *mortal* sin."

"Well, here's the rub, Mr. Vanderbilt, pardon the expression." Father Fairchild began. "I'm having a sexual relationship with a parishioner—"

"Father," Desmond interrupted, "even though you may consider this a *mortal sin*, can't God forgive you? Why are you both here with me, a trial defense attorney? We don't defend love. If you fall in love, love is love. As long as it's been for me, Father, I remember the Apostle Paul stating; 'love never fails.'"

"Mr. Vanderbilt, as I tried to explain...I shot her husband."

Desmond's eyebrows raised—his eyes widened, and he tensed to stand, then fell back in his chair. *It's not April Fool's Day, is it? This priest, the local Catholic Church, and the Roman Catholic Archdiocese need our firm's defense. Holy shit!* Desmond took a deep breath.

"Well, Father, shooting someone in and of itself doesn't mean the victim is dead, and you committed murder. Please go on," Desmond said.

"As I was saying, Mrs. Beall and I just had an immediate attraction to each other as soon as our eyes met while I served communion. I looked down, and she looked up as I placed the communion wafer to her lips. I couldn't believe my feelings. I tried desperately to fight my attraction to her and obey what I learned through the years. Mrs. Beall came to me for counseling and support because of her abusive husband. And it just happened. We couldn't stop. It was more than sex. I...we fell in love. I thought about leaving the church and she talked about leaving her husband."

"What kind of abuse did she suffer?" Desmond asked.

"Physical. He hit and kicked her, dragged her around by her hair."

"Did you witness this?"

"No, but I saw the bruises while we... Uh, she would cringe if I accidentally touched her bruises."

"Go on."

"Our love...affair I guess you'd call it, went on a little more than a year. We met in my office."

Monsignor O'Malley's groan resounded in the room.

"Monsignor," Desmond turned. "Control yourself or you will have to wait outside."

"Please, Father Fairchild, continue."

"We knew we had to stop meeting at the rectory, so we met at the motel and once at her house. That time her husband forgot something and came home. He walked in on us. He froze for a moment when he saw us naked, then he lunged at her, screaming; 'a priest! You're fucking a priest!' Cynthia, Mrs. Beall, struggled to get away from him. I jumped between them and she ran to the night table and opened the drawer. She reached in and pulled out her husband's gun. I tried to take it away from her, stop her from using it, and the gun went off."

"So, Father, did you pull the trigger or did Mrs. Beall? Guns don't *go off* by themselves. Someone has to pull the trigger. So, again, who pulled the trigger?"

"I...I...It had to be me. I pushed Mr. Beall down and grabbed at the gun Cynthia was holding with two hands. We struggled, but I wrestled the gun out of her grip. Cynthia screamed, 'Not this time, you bastard, not this time.' Mr. Beall got to his feet and ran toward us, grabbing at the gun. Now all of us struggled to possess

40

the gun. It went off. Mr. Beall fell to the floor and there we were, both of us standing together, naked, looking at him. We both had our hands on the gun. It happened so fast. I'm sorry. I did this. Cynthia did not shoot her husband."

"Are you positive, Father? It sounds like you're confused. Was anyone else in the house?"

"No. Their son is away at boarding school."

"And you're sure Mr. Beall is dead?"

"Mrs. Beall insisted I leave. We argued. I didn't want her to be alone, but...yes, he's dead."

"When did this take place, and where is his body?"

"It happened yesterday. His body is lying on the bedroom floor."

"He's still there? Where is Mrs. Beall?" Prying answers from this distraught man was like pulling hen's teeth, Desmond imagined. Father Fairchild was caught between feelings for his mistress and his religious commitment to the tenets of the Church, which embraced the Commandments, particularly *Thou shalt not kill.*

"She's at her home waiting for me. I told her I was coming to see you. She's alone with his body. I didn't want to leave. What should we do? What's going to happen to us? " Father Fairchild asked with the blank stare of shark eyes.

"We're going to go over your statement again. After we review this, you are going to say what I tell you to

41

say to the police. I believe this was self-defense from what you described. Mrs. Beall looked for the gun as a warning to stop her husband from beating her as he has in the past. When everyone struggled for the gun, in the confusion of the moment, it went off. We do not know who pulled the trigger. It could have been Mr. Beall. We will call the police and meet them at Mrs. Beall's house. I will speak with Mrs. Beall before the police arrive."

"Father, do not answer any questions without looking at me first, so I can tell you to answer or not. When they arrest you and Mrs. Beall, they will separate you and try to intimidate you. Do not answer any questions they are going to ask without me present. You tell them you will answer nothing without your attorney. Do you understand?"

"Yes, Mr. Vanderbilt. I know we're going to be arrested. I will face whatever punishment the law decides and I will have to face God's judgment."

"Father, you have your faith, Mrs. Beall by your side, and you have Desmond Vanderbilt."

Desmond turned the telephone toward Father Fairchild. "Call Mrs. Beall and tell her we are on our way and she's not to touch anything. Leave the gun exactly where it is. Rhonda, call the police in one hour and tell them to meet us.... What's the address, Father?"

CHAPTER 8

Desmond met with the D.A., following Mrs. Beall and Father Fairchild's arrests. They decided not to go forward with the Grand Jury. The Prosecutor linked Father Fairchild and Cynthia Beall's trial.

Desmond pushed for the defendants' constitutional rights for a speedy trial. That meant they had to go to trial within one hundred seventy-five days of arrest. The D.A. agreed, feeling it not only would save the State of Florida time and resources, it would reduce manpower hours his office must invest in two separate trials that could last for years with appeals.

The police charged Mrs. Cynthia Beall and Father Timothy Fairchild with *Involuntary Manslaughter,* which carried a sentence of fifteen years to life, if found guilty. Held in jail until the trial, proceedings began pursuant to the rules almost to the minute––one hundred and seventy days later.

All the local newspapers covered the trial, not only *The Miami Times, The Miami Daily, The South Florida Record,* but the newspapers of different ethnicities; *The Jewish Floridian, The Floridian Italian Bulletin, and Nuevo Diario De Miami. National News* and *National Newspapers* also sent reporters.

The *State of Florida vs. Beall and Fairchild* wasn't a lengthy trial. There were no witnesses, just the testimony of the defendants, the few police reports of the spousal abuse Mrs. Beall endured without arresting Mr. Beall, the Medical Examiner's autopsy report, and Police photos and reports of the crime scene. The jury could not agree upon who pulled the trigger—Cynthia Beall, Father Fairchild or Mr. Beall himself. The judge read the verdict, nodded, and handed the decision to the jury foreman.

We the Jury in the above-styled cause, in the United States District Court for the Southern District of the State of Florida, find the defendant, Timothy Fairchild Not Guilty of the offense charged in Count 1 of the indictment of Involuntary Manslaughter.

We the Jury in the above-styled cause, in the United States District Court for the Southern District of the State of Florida, find the defendant Cynthia Beall Not Guilty of the offense charged in Count 1 of the indictment of Involuntary Manslaughter.

The Courtroom burst into pandemonium. Flashbulbs from photographers' cameras lit up the room like the Fourth of July. The Judge pounded his gavel and called for sanity.

"ORDER! ORDER IN THIS COURT!" By now, the news reporters climbed over chairs and each other in their haste to find an unoccupied phone booth in the lobby to call their editor with a front-page scoop. The remaining publicity hounds finally settled for his Honor to continue.

"Is this verdict a unanimous decision reached by the Jury?"

"Yes, your Honor," replies the Jury Foreman.

"Before the court records the verdict, the court must determine with certainty that a unanimous verdict has been reached. I am going to poll the jury." And he began with Juror number one through and including Juror number twelve. All replied with a unanimous "Not guilty."

Thanking the jury for their service, the judge gave a short treatise after every verdict delivered to him by a jury.

"The Court thanks the Jurors for their time and service to their duty as citizens. Now, Timothy Fairchild, Mrs. Cynthia Beall, I must say that your love toward one another and for your God has brought you this far. Only your God and your conscience know for sure what happened in that room at that moment.

The Court pronounces you both *Not Guilty*. You are free to go. Court is now adjourned," and he struck the sound block.

A young boy with an older woman who sat together throughout the trial quietly left among the crowd.

The evening papers hit the stands. The front-page headlines carried a photo of the now defrocked Father Fairchild and Mrs. Beall in a lover's embrace.

Priest and Mistress NOT GUILTY in shooting of husband!

Who is behind the not guilty verdict?

God or the Devil himself!

CHAPTER 9

A celebration

Desmond, Libby and H-2 celebrated their victory and the receipt of their highest earned fee to date at the Cleopatra, a Gentleman's club where all of Miami's movers and shakers met. Many a deal took place there with just a handshake. Those included politicians, judges, lawyers, mobsters and anyone who held enough C-notes[3] in their hand.

The major attraction was Cleopatra, performing under the club's name, and was always the last act of the evening. Accounts from ancient Roman history depicted Cleopatra's use of her feminine charms to bewitch and influence powerful men and women of the ancient world.

When the MC announced, "Ladies and Gentlemen. The one you all have been waiting for, what the Roman critics wrote about Cleopatra, still stands today. Her wit

---

[3] C-note is slang for $100 bill for the Roman numeral "C" for 100 and the bill having a capital "C" in upper   left corner.

and intelligence were overshadowed only by her beauty and sexuality. Feast your eyes on... Cleopatra!"

You could hear a pin drop. Not a sound. No dishes rattled, not even a cough—complete silence.

The thirteen piece orchestra played sultry music as the curtain opened to a stage set that matched any New York Broadway play. Male dancers in breechclouts with greased chests dominated the stage, waving long, fluffy, ostrich feathers with no two alike. Behind the feathery natural plumage, Cleopatra emerged.

A magnificent specimen of a woman with flowing auburn hair in full regalia with the emblems, crown, and scepter that Cleo herself would have worn at her coronation. At this moment, lightning hit Desmond Vanderbilt.

Although Desmond had been to the club many times, he never paid attention to the entertainment. He had always conducted business, even during the show. But not tonight. Tonight was different. Cleopatra mesmerized him, and he knew he had to meet this beautiful woman. He would not take no for an answer. He didn't care what it took or how many markers he had to call in from anyone at his table or otherwise. He rubbed shoulders with powerful men, many of whom had joined him and his partners in celebrating Father Fairchild and Mrs. Beall's not guilty victory and were sitting at his table.

At Desmond's table was Miami's Mayor along with a congressional representative, municipal judge and the Editor of the *Miami Times*.

When Cleopatra ended her spectacular burlesque performance, just shy of wearing nothing but her birthday suit, Desmond excused himself and made his way backstage to meet the woman he knew he was going to marry. He walked past the open dressing rooms for the entertainers. He frequented the club and knew the owners. His path was clear. The bouncers never stopped him. They all knew Desmond—some were clients he had defended. The women were getting out of show costumes and into street clothes. They were accustomed to men entering their dressing rooms unannounced, accepting their nakedness with no reaction. They looked forward to going home, some to husbands or boyfriends. The women with children hurried so the baby sitter could leave, only to return the next night. This was just a well-paid job to them.

Cleopatra, as the club's headliner, had her private dressing room. Desmond tapped on the door.

"Who is it?" she asked.

"Desmond Vanderbilt."

"Just a moment, please." Lorraine opened the door in a red silk robe that matched the large glittering *RED STAR* on the door. Her flowing, dark ginger auburn hair hung loosely around her shoulders.

"Mr. Vanderbilt, come in. I've seen you in the audience. I hope you enjoyed tonight's show. I'm glad you stopped by to see me. If you don't mind, I'd like to run something by you. You know, something legal."

"Go ahead, please. I'm all yours," he said with fingers crossed.

49

CHAPTER 10

1868 Wilshire Court,

Palm Beach.

Judge Desmond Vanderbilt's Mansion.

L ester continued to question Lorraine. When did she find Desmond? His condition when she found him and where and what was she doing before she found him?

Lorraine raised her head to stare at Lester. "I remember the night Desmond introduced himself to me after the show. He was a gentleman, always, although I knew he wanted to get into my panties like every other man. But he was different. He was kind, without a blemish on his personality. He had a reputation of being a tough guy, making it the hard way. You know, Lester, like shooting craps and making your number the *hard way.*[4]"

---

[4] There are four even Points: the 4, 6, 8, and 10. When one of those rolls as a pair, it is considered to have rolled "hard." When they don't land as a pair, it is considered "easy." A Hardway is betting that the dice will land "hard" before they land "easy" or before a 7 is rolled.

"Oh, I know that game all too well. I've rolled snake eyes quite a few times. Remember, I have two ex-wives."

"Well, he rolled those dice right into my heart. We fell in love from our first meeting over twenty years ago." Lorraine's tears streamed down her face. She didn't wipe them away, and her streaking mascara left black lines on her cheeks. She continued to sip her vodka martini and smoke her cigarette. Lester pulled his snowy white initialed handkerchief from his breast suit pocket, handing it to her.

"Sure, I'd see him in the audience with his partners and guests, but never like that night he came to my dressing room.

"I dropped a few hints for him to make his move, but he remained a gentleman. That kind of man you didn't see often in those days or even today. We talked for hours, then went for breakfast. He was brilliant. He persuaded the owners of the club to give me ten percent ownership without paying one thin dime and, the best part...he wanted nothing in return. Well, you know what I mean, Lester. He wanted something, but he didn't expect me to *put out* for his help. He wanted me as a person, my heart, not just my body. I fell in love," she said again. "Desmond was a smooth operator who became my Mark Antony.

You know, Lester, the club owners on paper were not the real club owners who you never saw behind the curtain. Those men were ruthless. None of them cared about or for you. All they cared about was using the showgirls and making money, lots of it. Desmond stood up to them. He knew they would have to come to Vanderbilt, Harper, and St. James eventually. So why not cozy up to them? You know, one hand..."

"Sure, Lorraine. It washes the other. I used whatever I could with my snitches when I was on the Force. You have to because it works to your advantage."

"Yes, it does." Lester and Desmond knew how to work a win-win for everyone. "Those mobsters loved Desmond. They trusted him. They considered him their consigliere. You know that's what they called him–their advisor. He put them on a huge retainer besides his firm's hourly and expense billing. When the expenses reached a certain amount, they refilled the coffers over and over. That arrangement amounted to hundreds of thousands of dollars.

They invited Desmond to their home for an Italian Sunday homemade meal with their families. The only thing missing at these meals were the men's mistresses. After a while, I went with him. It was crazy, Lester. At home, they were devoted husbands and fathers. When they did business, they were ruthless and would throw you to the gators in the Everglades without batting an eyelash."

"Lorraine, you must call Libby and H-2."

"You're right, Lester. I'm going to."

"Now, Lorraine. Where's the phone? We're going to call them now."

"They're rarely in the office these days. The firm grew to one hundred attorneys by defending some of

Big Al's boys and the mob families. Vanderbilt, Harper and St. James have offices in Miami, New York and Chicago. Their reputation spread quickly as the top defense attorneys in the country with magazine spreads and newspaper headlines. I have Libby and H-2's private numbers in Desmond's study."

"I'll get them. Stay put."

"Lorraine, earlier you said, 'Looks can deceive.' What did you mean?"

"Let me tell you, Desmond, Libby and H-2 did not turn down any business no matter how small the crime or how big it was, man or woman. They knew starting out it would be that way with long grueling days lasting into the wee hours, Saturdays and Sundays, poring over law books, research for upcoming cases. Desmond convinced the newspapers to print his open-door policy for criminals. He once made the headlines in dozens of newspapers by offering to get Bonnie and Clyde light jail sentences if they met with him. It never happened. Bonnie and Clyde, that is, but it built their firm name as top defense attorneys. Criminals flocked in. They made deals that brought them big money."

"I remember that headline. It drew a lot of attention, particularly from the cops who hated him for his skillful defense in getting criminals off with light sentences, and many with acquittals."

"You know the game. Cops arrest the criminals; defense attorneys get them off. Once, the D.A. accused their law firm of taking $10,000 in stolen cash as a legal fee from the brother of one of the club owners. The cops arrested him for robbing a bank in Ft. Lauderdale. He paid the firm with the money he stole. There was no evidence that Desmond's defense was an aberration. I said looks can deceive because, as rich as we are, Desmond's success did not make him happy.

"Desmond wanted to serve on the Florida Supreme Court, but after they overlooked him a few times, he felt they were pushing him aside. He knew the process. The Governor had to appoint him to serve the first year. Then his retention would be up to the people of the state who chose judges by direct election. He knew he had to pay back the people who had helped him, and he did for a long time. But he didn't want to owe any favors when he was sworn in to the Florida Supreme Court. He earned his appointment, but some of his former contacts felt Desmond still owed them and they came at him as fast as a hard ball thrown by a New York Yankee's pitcher.

"The list of people that would want Desmond dead is extensive, and it includes the cops. He refused to grant more favors to people he had already paid back. He felt he'd paid all the favors he owed. I guess someone didn't agree or didn't like what he did or wouldn't do."

"So, Lorraine, from that statement, I take it you didn't kill your husband?"

Lieutenant Walker interrupted. "Mrs. Vanderbilt, I have to take you to the station. I'm sorry, at a time like this, but we have an investigation to conduct and you have to make a statement."

"Her attorneys are on the way. I'll be sure they meet her there." Lester leaned into Lorraine to whisper; "Don't worry and say nothing on your ride to the station or while you are there until Libby and H-2 arrive."

"Let me drive her, Ron."

"Caine, you know the drill. I can't allow that. I'm sorry, Mrs. Vanderbilt. I'll drive you myself."

CHAPTER 11

Lester moved to the crime scene to look around more closely since the Palm Beach Police were packing up. The coroner removed the body and Lorraine was on her way to the Palm Beach Police HQ. He wanted to look further; the room was too sterile. Almost staged.

He wanted to believe Lorraine had nothing to do with her husband's murder, and, from what she told him, he didn't believe it was a suicide. Vanderbilt made a lot of enemies, defending the low lives that slithered along the ground like the evil serpent from the Garden of Eden. But Lorraine never answered him directly.

There would be a rush on Desmond's autopsy to determine cause of death and rule out suicide. There always was on high-profile cases. However, here in this room was physical evidence to supplement the report and reveal the truth. Lorraine said Desmond was not fully on board with continuing to return favors he felt he already had paid and that created enemies. But Desmond had been a very logical, competent person with one of the most brilliant legal minds in the country. This, Lester thought, proved Desmond did not commit suicide. Lester saw the crime scene cop stick a pencil in the gun barrel and raise it to place it in the evidence bag. That was the right way to handle the gun. It should assure the fingerprints that came back would rule out Desmond and reveal another shooter

When it boils down to it, both the jury and the judge render sentences according to the facts, and facts are hard evidence found at the crime scene, supplemented by witnesses. However, here, there were no witnesses. At least, Lester hoped that excluded Lorraine.

"Mr. Caine, the Lieutenant said you can stay," said a cop from the CSI team. "I packed us up and we're ready to boogie. The crime scene tape will be up for a few days and there will be uniforms sitting out front all night. We will be back tomorrow. Lieutenant said to call him with anything you come up with."

"Ten–four." Lester waited to hear the door close before he began his search—moving things, looking for whatever he thought might be relevant. He could see evidence of the technicians' search by the dust on everything. It was standard procedure to look in all the drawers and closets and in the attic. No basements in Florida, unlike New York, which saved time and manpower. Lester knew the crime scene search unit had not looked everywhere. Evidence could be concealed.

He took his time, slow and methodical, opening drawers and moving things—in the drawers, on shelves, and in closets. He tapped the walls for hidden panels and safes, looked under lamps and behind paintings. Lester whistled softly. *Some of these by the likes of Paul Gauguin and Pierre-Auguste Renoir are worth tens of thousands of dollars.* Each painting hung to show it to its advantage. Lorraine had the best Palm Beach decorators at her beck and call.

Lester never let on to anyone that he studied art and knew the worth of an artist and his paintings. So, he concluded Vanderbilt's murder wasn't an art thief or a burglary. Nothing seemed to be missing or disturbed. Lester kept thinking of a targeted hit. Slowly, he continued, carefully examining, looking for clues that might be important, clues that weren't apparent. Then he found it.

Taped to the bottom of a drawer was a large manilla envelope. *Ah! Bingo! Why wasn't this, whatever it is, in the safe? Because Lorraine has the combination and Desmond was keeping it from her.*

Finally, he was satisfied both the search the Palm Beach Police team had conducted and his private search was complete, particularly now that he had something the police didn't have and might never have, depending on the contents.

Securing his find under his belt in the back of his pants, he checked that his suit jacket covered it. He said goodbye to the uniformed cops who guarded the crime scene as standard procedure dictated and returned to his office.

CHAPTER 12

Clematis Street.

Louise had a stack of messages on her desk to hand Lester when a woman walked through the door, refusing to state her business with Lester or whether she wanted to hire Lester Caine Investigations.

Louise interrupted Lester as he was about to open the manilla envelope he'd brought from the night table in Vanderbilt's bedroom. An oversight many police detectives had overlooked.

"Mr. Caine," Louise buzzed Lester's intercom. "There's a Mrs. Wanamaker here to see you. She just arrived." This was Louise's code for saying this person didn't have an appointment.

Lester quickly glanced at his appointment book, confirming there wasn't a Mrs. Wanamaker scheduled.

"Show her in, Louise," he said, knowing she would roll her eyes. Louise hated that Lester welcomed anyone who walked through the door.

Lester stood, his six-foot frame impressive. He extended his hand.

"I'm Lester Caine. I hope this introduction will be beneficial to you, Mrs. Wanamaker." Lester felt her warm handshake ooze welcome. "Please come in," gesturing for her to enter his private domain.

Roslyn Wanamaker was a classy dame. She wore a full black skirt and white waist-cinching jacket—Christian Dior's new silhouette design, redefining the American woman. She accessorized with what Lester called the widow's hat—a Schiaparelli black felt wide brim with a lace veil. This was a Palm Beach lady, and this *lady* did not buy off the rack. Behind that veil was a beautiful youthful face, although Lester took her to be mid-fifties. Her posture and deportment suggested a youthful countenance with a few lines that gave her the mark of distinction. She was stunning.

Louise sniffed. She wondered if Lester would give her a tumble if she dressed like that, the way he had other women who surround him.

"Will there be anything else, Mr. Caine?" addressing Lester as usual in front of clients. "Would you like coffee, *Mrs.* Wanamaker?"

"No, thank you."

"That will be all for now, Louise. Please close the door." Although eventually she would know all the details of each case, she loved to hear the details firsthand.

"Mrs. Wanamaker, what do you think I can help you with? I don't do cheating husbands or crawl around the hedges to take photos for evidence in divorce settlements."

"I know that, Mr. Caine. That's why I am here. I'm familiar with your reputation. I've read in the newspapers about your prowess as an investigator. You, Mr. Caine, are a paragon of knightly honor, even though you've been divorced twice."

"I'm impressed that you've done your due diligence. You would make a talented investigator yourself. Why do you need me?"

"Thank you, Mr. Caine. My meager resources can only do so much and they're not as extensive as yours."

Eyeing this lovely woman sitting within arm's reach, Lester indulged a quick thought to where he would like his extensive resources to be at this moment.

"I believe my husband is trying to kill me."

After twenty-five years as a hard-boiled Detective on NYC's mean streets, nothing really shocked Lester—not even Judge Vanderbilt lying on the floor oozing blood and brain matter on the Persian carpet from a bullet in his head, or the raging battle where a small part of him stayed behind when he left the Dominican Republic. He never brought his work home to either of his ex-wives. He often thought maybe he should have. *Then they would have understood when I worked around the clock—no sleep for twenty-four hours—and meeting with hookers and snitches.* Instead, he stared into the bottom of a Jim Beam Bourbon glass like so many other cops who didn't bring the job home. That's how Lester justified being a decorated cop.

"Would you like a drink, Mrs. Wanamaker? You seem a little frazzled."

"I, I, yes," dabbing her eyes with the handkerchief he handed her. "I would like a drink. Thank you."

Lester poured two fingers in each glass, suggesting they move to the more comfortable sitting area to ease her tension.

"Now, Mrs. Wanamaker, tell me about your husband, and don't leave out any details, even though you feel they are not important. You don't mind if I record this, do you?" Lester always asked, but never waited, pushing the start button.

"No, no, I don't mind. My husband, although you don't do cheating husbands, has a mistress. He is a prominent vascular surgeon at Florida General. If we divorce, he must pay me half of everything. I have the best divorce attorneys in Miami on retainer. He cannot escape without paying me every cent I deserve after thirty years of marriage. The only way out for him would be for me to die. Please say you will help me. Name your price, Mr. Caine."

"Mrs. Wanamaker, I charge two-hundred fifty dollars a day plus expenses."

Roslyn set down her drink and opened her purse. She took out her checkbook. "Here is a five-thousand-dollar retainer. This is a start. Wayne doesn't know about this account." She raised her glass, waiting for Lester's response.

Lester nodded.

"Cheers, Mr. Caine. Thank you."

"Alright, Mrs. Wanamaker, let's get to work. Stop me if you must. Your husband, Wayne, Doctor Wanamaker, a prominent surgeon, is having an affair. You feel he would rather kill or have you killed than pay you half of what the two of you own. How much are we talking about...roughly?"

"With our house, cars, jewels, his practice, stocks and bonds, just north of $1,000,000–give or take. Probably more give."

Lester thought he should have waited to tell her his fees.

"Mrs. Wanamaker, I wouldn't want to give up $500,000, but you haven't given me anything to go by except your husband has a mistress."

"I found this," pulling out a business card and handing it to Lester.

Mercenaries[5] and Guns for Hire

Leave First Name & Telephone Number Only

MI 5-7348

Lester read the information off the card into the recorder.

"This still does not show Doctor Wanamaker wants to have you killed. Listen, I'll check out these guns for hire. They, he, whoever, have a Miami telephone

---

[5] Mercenary is a person who cares only about money and would be willing to behave unethically to get it.

number and probably a Miami location for easy international access. I'll dig into it. On the surface, Mrs. Wanamaker, I see your concern. You must return this card to wherever you found it."

"I feel as though I'm being followed, Mr. Caine. You must know how that feels. You can actually feel someone's presence lurking, the itchy feeling on your back. I'm afraid to start my car. I've read about mobsters blowing up cars. I'm frightened, Mr. Caine."

"I see. Is Mr. Wanamaker tied to mobsters? Did he borrow money from a loan shark? Is he in debt because of his mistress? Has he set her up in her own place? Is he paying for a love nest? Any bills coming in the mail you don't recognize?"

"All our bills go to his office and he pays them there. Wayne was at a medical convention and I called his room one evening. A woman answered. I hung up."

"I see. Do you know this mistress, her address, where she may work?"

"I know her name...Millie Sparks. She works at Burdines Department Store in the men's suit department."

"That makes it easy. Another, Mrs. Wanamaker?" lifting the Jim Beam bottle of bourbon. "You need protection twenty-four hours a day, seven days a week, at an additional cost."

"I think that could be arranged, Mr. Caine," she said, sipping her second drink. "Mr. Caine," she said, less sure of herself, "do you think I need a gun? Can you get me a gun?"

"No, and No!"

CHAPTER 13

Palm Beach.

Lester received word that Lorraine was at the Floridian Hotel on South County Road on Palm Beach Island where many celebrities vacationed during their hiatus from movie making so they could be undisturbed on the hotel's private beach. Desmond's former partners, Libby St. James and H-2, accompanied Lorraine.

Lester instructed Louise to get hold of *Scarecrow,* his Field Assistant Gloria Saville, to begin immediately what she did best–dig up information on Roslyn and Wayne Wanamaker, Millie Sparks, and the Miami guns for hire.

Gloria was a classy dame who could be a stealth beauty or a hard nose bitch. She knew how to play the game and play it to the full. She'd done summer stock and sometimes filled in at the local playhouse theater. Gloria was a freelance Private Investigator who did work for Lester and attorneys around town. She had a reputation of a gal who could get it done and knew how to handle herself. She assumed many disguises, thus known as *Scarecrow.* Gloria had a few first-place trophies in Regional Jujutsu tournaments after leaving the US Army, where she served as an intelligence officer and master cryptologist. [6]

Lester drove his Cadillac down the long palm tree lined drive leading to the Floridian Hotel. Valets in pristine uniforms and white gloves ran to open car doors, greeting guests at the entrance.

"Put the top up when you park her. You know Florida's changeable weather. It could rain in a moment," Lester said, stepping out and handing the valet a five spot. "Put her in a special place while you're at it."

"Oh, yes, sir. Thank you. I'll take good care of her, don't you worry."

"I'm so glad you're here, Lester." Libby greeted him and handed him a drink before he sat. "We're glad you made Lorraine call us. That was the smart thing to do in this situation. We are in shock. It's surreal."

"Good to see you, Lester," H-2 chimed in.

"You too, H-2."

"We're working a few cases we could use you on. Some big ones."

---

[6] A cryptologist is a person who works to decipher hidden language, crack secret codes, and find ways to protect information. An individual in this line of work may help to create codes the military can use to communicate in secret,

"You know where to reach me, H-2. Where is Lorraine?"

"She took a sedative and is sleeping," Libby said. "She'll be alright here for a day or so. I've hired a service to clean the house as soon as Lieutenant what's his name says they can get in there. I'm hoping he will release it tomorrow or the next day."

"His name is Lieutenant Walker. What has Lorraine told you?"

"Not a thing. She is in shock," H-2 answered.

"What about at the Police station?" Lester asked.

"We both were by her side in the interrogation room, Lester. She explained she was in the bedroom when she heard a loud noise or a rumbling and came downstairs. She found Desmond just where he lay. At first, she thought it was suicide and wondered why he'd do it," H-2 said.

"She saw the gunshot wound to the head and knew he was dead, so she called the police. Lorraine knew not to touch anything. They'll pull her *RAP Sheet*," Libby said.

"That's old news. They won't find any violence," Lester scoffed. He didn't let on he and Lorraine had a history back to New York when he was her arresting officer. "Well, the good thing is Lorraine didn't kill him. She told me their housekeeper, Rosemary, was off. Have you been able to reach her?"

"Haven't tried. She said nothing about the housekeeper. I assume the police asked her. Not sure, Lester."

"Try to find her, will you, Libby? She should stay here with Lorraine."

"Sure, Lester, as soon as Lorraine gets up. I can stay with her until the housekeeper gets here."

"We've got our work cut out for us. Did you see what the police took with them?" Libby asked, raising her eyebrows.

"No, Libby, can't say that I did. Is there something I'm missing?" Lester thought it a strange question of all things to ask.

"No, no. Not at all. You know, sometimes the cops think something may be evidence and it isn't at all."

"Just the gun...that's all I saw." *She must know something Desmond may have that might be incriminating. I've got to get back to that envelope.* "Where's the phone?"

"In the bedroom," H-2 answered.

Lester got up only to hear Libby say, "Lester, you'll wake her."

"You said she took a sedative. She won't wake up. I just remembered something important." Lester dialed the office number.

"Louise," Lester whispered, "it's Lester. Put the envelope I left on my desk in the safe," and he hung up and rejoined Libby and H-2.

"Libby, H-2, what can you tell me? I know Desmond had to have made enemies defending criminals that should have gone to prison, but he got them off. Being a judge too. Did he receive any threats over the years?"

"Of course, all of us received threats. Even the office staff who have nothing to do with our winning case after case received threats. What does a secretary or mail clerk have to do with anything?"

"C'mon, Lester. You're a retired New York City Detective. You know about that. We even got threats from your brothers in blue. We successfully represented a lot of criminals, many of them were charged with crimes, but we got them off because of sloppy police work. I don't blame them, but it's on them. You must have witnessed that yourself during your career. They're idle threats," H-2 sounded off.

"Maybe, maybe not, H-2. Did you keep a file on the threats?" Lester asked.

"You know we did, Lester. I can get it for you," Libby answered without being prodded.

"Yes, courier it to my office. I want to look at it. Does anyone know of any threats Desmond received while sitting on the bench? Will you subpoena the court for his files—"

"Who's there?" a groggy voice interrupted Lester.

"We're in the sitting room, Lorraine. Me, H-2, and Lester," Libby answered, going to the bedroom. "Lorraine, why don't you shower? You'll feel better. I packed some clothes for you. And Lorraine, I need contact information for Rosemary, the pool service, and the gardener. We want to speak to them. So do the Police."

CHAPTER 14

The 1930s was the decade that brought *the* Art Déco architectural design to Miami Beach. Investments by the benefactor Henry Doherty helped keep Miami and Coral Gables afloat during tough times. Miami continued to expand its transportation and infrastructure to support growth. With that came corruption and kickbacks for awarding contracts.

This was a period most of America wanted to forget. However, this era provided a lot of opportunities for South Florida and the criminals that flocked there.

The local law and FBI kept a constant vigil on the milieu for the comings and goings of the entourage, both men and women, into Al Capone's mansion on Palm Island. Imagining all that went on behind closed doors or at poolside on his property frustrated Law Enforcement. Criminals took advantage of coming to South Florida. They knew the heat would be on the mansion and not on them. They were unlikely to turn up on Miami's police blotter.

The law firm of Vanderbilt, Harper and St. James became a revolving door for this unsavory element, getting many criminals a not guilty verdict or case dismissal, claiming the proceedings violated their Fourth Amendment rights. Many times, the crime was so public and the cops wanted the collar so badly, they tossed out procedure, taking a chance to see what charges would stick to the wall.

Most arrests did not stick to the great *Blue Wall because* of unreasonable searches or those conducted without signed warrants. Although Desmond, Libby and H-2 fraternized with the politicians, judges and city officials, they created enemies behind the blue line. The trio were a powerful force with national contacts from the coalition they were part of that was combating the ban on alcohol and their part in helping to repeal the Eighteenth Amendment. In addition, the beat cops hated them and wanted revenge, but knew they couldn't touch Desmond, Libby or H-2.

Many cops could not forget the slime of the earth that slithered past the prison cells where they belonged but were free because of Vanderbilt, Harper and St. James. Lester's information came right from the horse's mouth—Lorraine Vanderbilt. This compounded the reason Desmond's brains were splattered onto the imported Persian rug. From this, Lester knew any one of many could have killed him.

"Lester, Lieutenant Walker is on the line," Louise announced over the intercom.

"Ron, what do you have?"

"ME's report came back. No prints on the gun or anywhere else. Real clean with the exception of a footprint found outside the French doors. We took a plaster cast and are checking to discover the brand of shoe. The gun grip was stippled. [7] and the serial number filed off. No signs of forced entry."

"None of the neighbors saw anything or any strangers," Walker continued. "And Mrs. Vanderbilt wasn't expecting any deliveries. The autopsy shows no drugs, alcohol, or substance abuse. The ME said if the Judge shot himself in the head, there would be an abrasion ring showing where he pressed the barrel to his head at the point of entry. There was the suggestion of an oval shape at an acute angle to the entrance to the right temple, with the barrel at least six inches away. The ME listed Desmond Vanderbilt's death as a homicide. Between you and me, Lester, this has all the elements of a professional hit. The ME said the weapon was a .22 caliber. You know what that means!"

"Up close and personal. And he used a silencer."

"That's right. Here are a few more tidbits for your quiver. The blood spatter shows the shooter was right-handed. Mrs. Vanderbilt told us the Judge was left-handed. We have a murder, Caine. I'm open for anything you can offer."

"Thanks Lieutenant, I'll get back to you. I have some pokers in the fire."

---

[7] Gun grip (handle) stippled is when the handle is modified from the manufacturers issue to fit the shooter's hand for a better grip.

"I figured you might. Talk to you soon."

Lester hung up the phone, deep in thought. *All the indications of a professional hit. What did you do, your Honor?*

CHAPTER 15

Clematis Street

Louise set the morning paper on Lester's desk after doing the crossword puzzle in ink, which she usually knocked out within fifteen minutes while enjoying her first cup of Joe.

She also read her and Lester's horoscope.

Lester didn't mind. He was interested only in the news that was fit to print, which excluded the daily satire cartoon or the Sunday comic strips, except for Dick Tracy. [8] Lester considered the tough, intelligent detective his alter ego.

Louise heard Lester's steps approaching the office door. Before he opened it all the way, she greeted him, always positive. "Good mornin', Lester. It's a new day with a lot of good things that are going to happen."

---

[8] Dick Tracy is an American comic strip originally, Plainclothes Tracy, a tough and intelligent police detective created by Chester Gould. It made its debut on Sunday, October 4, 1931 in the Detroit Mirror.

"Good morning, Louise. That coffee smells so good. You know how to get me going in the morning, don't you?"

Lester, you don't know how I would love to get you going and not just in the morning, Louise's mind rambled.

"Today will be a good day for you, Lester."

"Okay, I'll bite."

I wish..."Your horoscope says since you're a Gemini, ruled by Mercury, and you are in the third house, your moon is moving through Gemini. That means this week you're easily distracted and it will be hard for you to focus. So, Lester, you have a lot going on. Listen to the Astrologer's advice. Take a gander at the morning headlines. That will put you on your toes."

Lester put his hot cup of coffee down, which he so enjoyed, only to be jolted by the headline staring him square in the face. There it was. Louise left the morning paper on his desk out of order since she read it earlier. He read the headline over and over, thinking maybe his horoscope might be right... this time.

Judge Desmond Vanderbilt Murdered in his Palm Beach Mansion. Mrs. Vanderbilt, a Former Exotic Dancer Taken into Custody

Additional details, page 3.

"Oh, shit!" Lester groaned.

"Everything all right, Lester?" Louise called with a smirk.

"Jesus H. Christ, Louise, I can't believe how these bastard reporters get this information so fast and how they spin it to sell newspapers. It must be all over the AP. Do they pay somebody under the table for fresh information?"

"Lorraine hasn't been on stage or set foot in the Club Cleopatra since she and the Judge married over twenty years ago. They did not take her into custody. Lieutenant Walker asked her to go downtown and give her statement. She went to the Police station voluntarily with her attorneys. This headline is bullshit, and John Q. Public buys it hook, line and sinker."

"Could be, Lester. Just remember what your horoscope said. Don't get distracted or someone could pull the wool over your eyes."

"Hmm," Lester said. *Maybe this dame isn't so ditzy after all.* "Let me see that horoscope bullshit. "

"Please get me that envelope from the safe," he asked after his rant.

Lester removed his trusted Swiss Army knife from the top desk drawer, the one he'd had with him during his four-year tour in the Navy. He inserted the blade to open the sealed envelope, careful not to tear any of the contents. He thought it might be in-depth information on a criminal he had represented, or maybe inside information on the King Fish himself, directly from Palm Island, or one of his henchmen. Lester's brow furrowed. It had to be damning for the Judge to conceal it from Lorraine. He turned the envelope over, examining it for writing or distinguishing marks. He had no idea what to expect. The missive was just a plain large manilla envelope with a clasp and sealed.

Louise buzzed him on the intercom. "Lester, I have Scarecrow on the phone."

"Thank you. Put this envelope back in the safe."

Louise retrieved the envelope and carried out Lester's request, desperately wanting to open the envelope. She knew it had to be something important for him to keep it in the safe.

CHAPTER 16

Hialeah

Lester spotted Gloria Saville, aka the Scarecrow, sitting in her favorite spot in the Grandstand under cover seating at Hialeah Park, reading The Daily Racing Form.

She oozed self-confidence, reliability and her attire pure class, as usual—large brim white straw hat with a black ribbon band to match her black and white polka dot spaghetti strap summer dress. Lester was a leg man and his eyes appreciated her long crossed legs down to her black patent leather sling back heels. She wore large lensed sunglasses, just like her favorite actress, Lauren Bacall. Gloria's intelligence and sexual allure invited any man to stare, even if accompanied by his wife.

Scarecrow loved this race track with its landscaped gardens of native flora and fauna, and the infield lake stocked with beautiful pink flamingos. She held many of her business meetings here, inconspicuous, just another racing fan. Lester rolled his racing form into the semblance of a baker's rolling pin.

"Ah, Lester, good to see you," Gloria patted the seat next to her.

"You are ravishing, as always, Gloria. Who do you like?"

"I'm going with the favorite, Mello Baby. Now that you've checked out my legs, look at the board," she answered with a coquettish grin, handing Lester her binoculars. "You better make the window. It's close to post time."

Back in his seat, just as the bell rang, the announcer declared all windows closed; the bugler trumpeted the traditional *Boots and Saddle* call for riders up to exit the paddock and proceed to the track for the post parade and warm-up before loading the starting gate.

Announcer: "There's the bell and they're off..."

This was the best time for Lester and Gloria to talk business. The crowd jumped to their feet, shouting at the jockeys, shaking their racing forms, screaming encouragement or obscenities.

Some argue that this apogee of human intelligence would make their ticket magically appear as an across-the-board winner. Not considering the fact that the thoroughbred might be out for a romp, or a few ticks off the last few weeks of training, or it might be a mudder. Thoroughbreds have their off days, as do the jockeys sitting atop these 1,000 pound animals.

Announcer: "There it is, Ladies and Gentlemen, a blanket race right to the end. Hold those tickets. Wait for the photo finish... It's official. The winner is Mello Baby, paying nine to one with a twenty-dollar payout for the win, five to two paying seven dollars for place, and two to one for show paying six dollars. The next race will start in twenty minutes. Plenty of time to place your bets and..." drifting off into the airwaves.

They made their way to the window to cash out their winning tickets before heading to the bar.

"Gloria, anything on Roslyn and Wayne Wanamaker or the Miami gun for hire?"

"I've got some dirt on the mistress, Millie Sparks. Get this, Lester. She is a widow. Her husband died suspiciously. There was no proof of foul play. The death certificate ruled it an accidental death.

However, the police report hints at it not being an accident. Her husband was working under the car in their garage when the jack slipped, crushing him. She collected $100,000."

"No shit. So, why is she working in the men's suit department at Burdine's?"

"Here's the rub, Lester. She lost every penny, investing in fraudulent stocks that went south. Her then boyfriend was arrested for securities fraud and is doing a nickel. Can you imagine losing a hundred large? I guess Miss Karma came around with a fuck you."

"Securities fraud? That's five years– easy time, Gloria. He'll do it standing on one leg. Probably get out early for good behavior."

"So, she's been around the block and is probably on track to get Roslyn Wanamaker killed. She would then marry the doctor, and who knows her plans for him. She is a black widow, for sure. I have nothing else at the moment. "

Lester signaled the bartender. "Vodka martini for the lady–stirred, and Jim Beam neat with ice on the side."

"Impressive, Lester, you always remember. I love a strong man in charge."

Lester thought, *easy to remember you and Lorraine.* The conversation lent itself to the vicissitudes of the PI biz—far from the mundane lives of the everyday ham and eggers. The Mediterranean Lounge featured The Sonny Abbott Trio, bringing them to the dance floor in slow embraceable fashion.

Finishing the third round, Gloria gently set her martini glass down and laid her hand on Lester's thigh. "Your place or mine?"

CHAPTER 17

The Hacienda Arms Apartments.

The morning sun peeked through the partially drawn curtain like a spotlight hitting Sinatra on center stage at the Paramount Theater. Gloria shuffled the sheets and turned toward Lester, placing her nakedness next to his, running her fingers through his chest hair, making curlicues.

"Good morning, Lieutenant. You're still as good as ever. I love that tattoo of Lady Justice every time I see it. The best part is the word *wisdom* you added along the bottom."

"Good morning to you. I'm glad you like it," Lester smirked. "You're just as beautiful when you wake up as you were the night before." Lester closed his eyes and took a deep breath, taking in her scent.

"I'm liking it just fine. I'm going to show you exactly how much I like it as soon as I pee. Be right back, big boy. Don't go anywhere."

"I'm right behind you."

"Oh, no." Gloria jumped up, throwing the sheet over Lester's head. "Ladies first, just like last night."

Lester lived at The Hacienda Arms Apartments, a gracious five story building that flowed with old world Spanish Renaissance architectural charm. It housed thirty-six apartments and was once a first-class hotel for visitors of means to Palm Beach. Lesters's one-bedroom apartment with a balcony overlooked the marina where the likes of many a ship that sailed from distant ports tied up.

It was perfect for him and his guests, always clean, thanks to a twice a month cleaning lady he employed. Lester was a man who liked a place for everything and everything in its place, even his women. Supposedly, Yvonne Bulette, a famed Paris Madam, ran a bordello out of this one-time top hotel, The Chesterfield, now the Hacienda Arms Apartments. If only the walls could talk, what would they shout? What would the walls in Lester's apartment reveal? It didn't matter. Lester had his own ghosts stacked up in the closet that could spew many a tale.

Lester got to his office early, which was unusual. He fiddled with the coffeepot, then decided to leave it.

"Lester, good morning. Don't even try. Get away," Louise, two steps behind him shooed, waving her hands. "I'll get the coffee going. Give me a minute." She set down the box of donuts. "There's a message from Lieutenant Walker on your desk. It came in late yesterday afternoon."

"Thank you," he said, already reading. 'Housekeeper off on Thursdays with an alibi. Gardener and pool service come twice a month on different days. They checked out as to their whereabout that day.'

86

"Good morning, Louise," the mailman greeted . "Got ya a special delivery today. Ya need to sign for it—right here," he pointed "Tell Lester I said hello."

"Sure thing, Harry. Help yourself to a donut."

"Lester, looks like H-2 and Libby sent you the file you've been waiting for," she called out, tucking it under her arm and bringing Lester his coffee.

"When did that envelope arrive?"

"Just now. Harry said to say hello."

"Back at you, Harry," he mumbled," brushing him off.

The envelope was thinner than he expected, the return address Vanderbilt, Harper and St. James. The firm would not give up the Vanderbilt name on the Marquee. It was too valuable. Lester knew the envelope contained the file of threats Vanderbilt had received. His gut told him it would not be a house of horrors from the envelope's size as he slipped the pages from the mailer. A dozen sheets of paper with names, addresses and telephone numbers. They had referenced the police follow-up reports to the list at hand.

"Huh, I say they're probably idle threats. Let me go through them, Lester. I bet you thought the file would be this thick," holding her hands a foot apart. She reached to take them from him.

"Good idea, Louise. Get me Lorraine Vanderbilt and Roslyn Wanamaker on the phone. Lorraine first."

"Lorraine, it's Lester. How are you holding up?"

"I feel like my brain's in a fog. My Doctor gave me sleeping pills. The pills and vodka are getting me through. Everything's cleaned up here. Thank you for arranging that.

"Thank Libby. She arranged it."

"Where or what do we do from here?"

"There's nothing you can do at the moment, unless you have a probate attorney to start transferring assets to you.

Libby is helping me go through Desmond's papers, and she'll stay with me for a few days. Desmond was pretty organized, and he laid it all out in his will, life insurance, and instructions. He was..."

Lester heard her crying. "Lorraine, do you want me to come over?"

"Thank you, Lester. I'm okay," composing herself. "Libby is here now. We are going to make the funeral arrangements. I hope the ME releases Desmond soon. I miss him."

"H-2 and Libby and myself are on the police details," Lester hurried to continue, unable to think of any comfort to offer her. "Lieutenant Walker and his men are looking at all the angles. The gun came back clean, so we know, like you knew, it wasn't suicide. Nothing was out of order, no forced entry. Do you have an alarm?"

"No, we never got one. We never thought we'd need one living here."

"I'll call a company I do business with. They'll install one by tomorrow. Lorraine, you need to take care of you. Do you have family, a priest or rabbi you can call? You know you can always call me. You just can't leave town at the moment."

"Thank you, Lester. I was never a person for one God over another, or any church. I searched a few times, but vodka always appeared in place of any gods, mystical or otherwise."

"There is a police unit outside your house and will be there for a few days."

"Thank you, Lester. I want you to know I never thought for one second that Desmond would commit suicide, even though someone always pressured him to return favors for help he got to reach the bench. He started pushing back. He was confident his credentials were really what got him where he wanted. Sure, there were politics involved, but that's part of it. You know, I don't mean a political party. "

"I know exactly what you mean, Lorraine. One hand washes the other."

"That's it, Lester. Desmond never rested on his laurels or wanted any more favors. We'll talk. Anytime you feel you want to, please come. Thanks for calling. I will call you if I need you."

He heard the dial tone.

"Are you ready for me to call Mrs. Wanamaker?" Louise asked.

"Mrs. Wanamaker, it's Lester Caine. I have some information that supports your claim against Mr. Wanamaker's planning to kill you. His mistress is a dangerous person and considered a Black Widow."

"Oh, my God! I mean, I knew I was right. What do you mean, this bitch is a Black Widow?"

"It means she's a woman who kills her lovers. In this instance, it's her lover's wife... you! Her first husband died in a freak accident. The cops were suspicious, but could not prove she murdered him. He had a large life insurance policy. We can only presume that's the plan. Who knows, maybe she plans to marry Mr. Wanamaker after you're gone, then murder him."

"Her motive would be another life insurance policy your husband would take out, naming her the beneficiary. After her husband died, she got herself mixed up with another man who is now in prison."

"I knew it. That son-of-a-bitch and his whore! Why don't I just kill them both?" Roslyn asked.

Lester hoped it was a rhetorical question.

"Mrs. Wanamaker, please don't say that. Someone may take you seriously. Did you buy a gun?

"No! Should I get one? I wouldn't know how to use it. They scare me. When I asked you about that, you said; no. You said something about a woman like me needing protection around the clock. Can you do that?" she asked, seduction in her voice.

"Let's put the gun business aside for the moment. I've got to get you protection. One of my staff will start following you. I will let you know who and when, so they don't spook you. Are we clear?"

"Yes, Mr. Caine. I understand. You're in charge," she purred like a sex kitten. "I'll await your instructions. Thank you."

"Don't thank me yet, Mrs. Wanamaker."

CHAPTER 18

Palm Beach Police Headquarters

Lester made his way to the Palm Beach Police station just south of the Floridian Hotel on South County Road. The old-fashioned building housed the entire police force of just over one hundred officers, the Police Chief, Captain, and additional civilian office workers.

The long barrier island stretched sixteen miles in length and less than a mile wide. It was home to millionaires and some of the highest real estate values in the country. Lester smiled at the photo gallery of the Police Chiefs hanging on the lobby wall, thinking back on his days as a NYC Detective. The entire police force for Palm Beach numbered less than one shift at his old precinct. He knew the PBPD was not equipped to handle a murdered Judge.

The desk sergeant didn't care for private investigators. They didn't have to follow rules, and he didn't like that. The fact that Lester was a New York City transplant detective–a city slicker, was also not his cup of tea. He always gave Lester a tough time. Lester kept his cool, but it cost him.

He thought, *I hope Ron doesn't have to call in the FBI for assistance.* Only that thought and preventing the Feds from rolling over this department like a steamroller stopped him from exploding over the desk sergeant's demeanor.

"The Lieutenant will see you now, Mr. Caine," the desk sergeant said, speaking with a curled lip.

Man, would I love to knock that smirk off your mug just for fun. Lester ached to give rise to the situation.

"I know, I know. I apologize," Ron said. "Don't mind Bert. He's days away from retirement. His wife is forcing him to take it. What's this?" Ron asked as Lester handed him a sheaf of papers.

"Thought you'd like a copy of the threats His Honor got over the years. We—my staff and me—and the Miami Police followed them up, but you should know about them, anyway."

"Doesn't seem to be too many here, considering all the cases his firm has handled and some of the twisted noses he got off from prison terms. It's in line that victims' families might seek revenge. This seems a little light, considering. Maybe a few slipped through the cracks from the previous police reports, or he didn't report some. Vanderbilt must have been primary at thousands of trials. I'll look that up and make a comparison. Thanks, Caine. You can never be too sure."

Ron openly displayed his concern at no leads. Throwing the file on his desk, he didn't want to admit he was stumped. He hated to think of relinquishing the

93

case. Calling in the FBI was the last resort and would tarnish the Palm Beach Police force.

"Just so you know, Ron, I'm following up these threats as well. Although some of them have been years ago, you never know what gets stuck in a man's craw. Besides, it can take years for something to percolate inside a person, like a pressure pot before... BAM! Let's hope not. But to be on the safe side, I thought I'd share with you."

"Let's have a look," Ron opened the file. "I remember some of these trials. They should have resulted in lengthy sentences for these bastards! You know as well as I do, Caine, that "these people," (Ron crooked his fingers, using the quote signs), are a menace to society. And from the looks of it, the families want revenge plain and simple because Desmond got the criminals a not guilty verdict or very short jail terms. People in the life[9] hold no statutes of limitations, only their memories. Their credo is "we're coming for you and you will never know when or where.""

"Ron, we're not talking about criminals seeking revenge. It's the victim's families of the criminals that Desmond got off."

"I know. I'm speaking of the criminals that were Desmond's clients that he helped, who will not let go. If they find out who did this, whoever killed Desmond will pay one way or another by their hand because of

---

[9] In the Life is an expression meaning being in the life of crime.

what Desmond did for them. One killing could lead to another and we could witness the start of a war."

"We've got to get something to go on. I'm working on my end and I know you're working yours. I don't want you to call in the FBI. They will bust through your door and plow right over Sergeant Bert. They won't put up with his bullshit. Besides, His Honor was not a Federal Judge or going to be one. He was going to sit on the Florida Supreme Court. So, the Feds won't intervene unless they're called in. They don't interfere unless absolutely necessary. This is your baby, Ron."

"Now it's my turn: don't fuck this up. I will share with you anything and everything I come up with. I appreciate you bringing me in on this one."

"Well, you know she, Mrs. Vanderbilt, asked for you. This list is a start. I'm sure there must have been more."

"Keep this in mind, Ron. The Miami police have their reports in there and they did their due diligence. Their reputation is on the line. Now yours is going to be in question if you find anything after working this list." Lester wanted to put the pressure on Ron, pushing him to get one step ahead of the shoeshine.

"A lot of eyes see better. Maybe they overlooked something. Will the Vanderbilt, Harper and St. James firm check their files to show how many trials ended in not guilty or light sentences were doled out compared to this list?" Ron questioned.

"What you see is what you get unless we go to the archives. I can't imagine what those files look like. There must be thousands."

"Thanks, Caine. We'll get to work on this."

CHAPTER 19

Clematis Street

Louise had gone through the file of threats twice, making contacts and answering queries that a present investigation might connect to a murder, which terrified the hell out of them.

She gave Lester a solid explanation of the whereabouts of the person who had made the threat at the time of Desmond's murder. She also included the Miami Police follow-up reports and concluded, "There's nothing here. Nothing, nil, nada. I've gone over this file and the police records with a fine-tooth comb. Everyone on this list is a blowhard. They're just letting off steam. Trust me. These are angry family members whose loved ones were victims. They became victims again when the criminals who committed the crimes got off with not guilty or light sentences because of Desmond Vanderbilt, even those convicted of manslaughter."

"Good job, Louise. There's no fooling you. You filled in the blanks. So, we're back to zero on who could have murdered the Judge. It might be someone who never made the list of threats. It had to be a *hit*. No signs of a break-in or struggle and everything wiped clean. No shell casings. So, it was most likely a revolver. The *hit* man would not look for the spent shell. The ME said the slug was a .22, which means up close and personal. Whoever it was, got clean access"

I'd like you to pull a blindfold over my eyes and maybe handcuff me... Lester's imported *Old Bond Street* cologne tickled Louise's nose, sending her off in a wonderful daydream.

"Louise, are you alright? You look like you're off on some distant shore," Lester inquired.

"I'm good," Louise gave a chuckle.

"I'm thinking that Desmond's murderer had to be someone who knows about killing and crime scenes. He's familiar with the ins and outs of police procedure and how we work a crime scene."

"Lester, do you think a cop killed Desmond?" Lester's phone rang, startling Louise.

"Ahem," clearing her throat. "Lester Caine Private Investigations, how may I help you? Hold please." She covered the mouthpiece, whispering, "Lester, it's Scarecrow." She handed him the receiver and returned to her desk.

"Gloria?" Lester asked.

"Got some goods on our Miami Mercenary. Listen to this. These men, part of a mercenary unit called The Gurkhas, fought for the British in the Middle East, and the French in the colonies in French North Africa. The units were from three countries: Morocco, Algeria, and Tunisia during WWII. The Miami mercenaries worked for whoever paid the most. Today, these guys are carrying on what they do best, only by private invitation and for private exclusive assignments, whether here or abroad. I'm getting enough intel on them to get me in the door.

One of them came in contact with Dr. Wanamaker, through needing surgery to open up blocked arteries in his neck. They became friends since his condition required frequent follow-up. He's retired and behind the scenes while other mercs carry out contracts. It seems they are pretty stacked up. I can't imagine how many murders by these professionals go unsolved. From the looks of things, they're not afraid to stain their hands with blood. Dr. Wanamaker invited this guy to sit in on his poker game with his other buddies.

It seems the Doc is not a stuck-up son-of-a-bitch that prides himself on a country club membership, unlike Mrs. Wanamaker, who loves that lifestyle with her private tennis lessons and frequent spa appointments. His friends are not doctors and lawyers. His poker buddies are ordinary guys—the car salesman he purchased a car from for Mrs. Wanamaker, the jeweler where he bought a ring, his mailman, and the A&P Supermarket manager. The Doc is a typical guy in every sense except for planning a murder."

"Maybe it's a con. You know, to be an everyday guy to the common man," Lester questioned.

"Doesn't seem that way, Lester. Wayne Wanamaker is just what he seems—a highly sought-after vascular surgeon with common friends except for a contract hit man under the guise of a businessman. Meet Mr. Jean-Paul Laurent, the man behind the curtain and head mercenary gun for hire. He has a crew to take care of business."

"What does Laurent report to the IRS as his income?

"My informant told me, and don't laugh. You're not going to believe this. Winston Churchill forced General De Gaulle to end the French mandate, which helped nationalist Shukri al-Quwatli become Syria's President. It opened the door for Jean-Paul Laurent since he had all the ins as a mercenary to supply Syria with surplus war dry goods—uniforms, and body equipment for soldiers. And get this, Lester, what they want most of all are patent leather boots," Gloria hooted. "I guess they want the sun to reflect the shine in the desert," Gloria laughed.

"Jesus Christ, Gloria. You can't make this shit up. Anything more on his mistress?"

"Nope. Not a thing. She goes to work on her schedule, which changes from week to week. That's why she and the Doc can tryst on different days and times. They seem to have an affinity for none other than the Floridian Hotel."

"No shit!"

"What is it, Lester?"

"That's where Lorraine stayed for a few days after Desmond's murder."

"You may have passed the Doc and Millie in the lobby," Gloria chuckled.

"Gloria, good work. Keep digging. This is great stuff."

Lester heard the click followed by the dial tone, hesitated for a moment, then hung up. Gloria could be a heartbreaker, but she certainly knew how to be a ball buster. She got the job done and done right.

"What were you suggesting about a cop?" he called to Louise.

Strutting into his office, Louise perched on the edge of his desk, crossed her legs and faced him. She leaned over to straighten his tie.

Lester raised one eyebrow with a slight smile, encouraging her. "Thanks. I should get a tie clip. I never liked them."

"You were saying how the crime scene was clean, no sign of a break-in, no one saw any strangers or delivery trucks. The Vanderbilts' mail goes to a post office box, which the housekeeper picks up during the week. Mrs. Vanderbilt didn't hear any scuffle, just a thud when Desmond hit the floor. She didn't even hear a gunshot. So, the killer had to use a silencer. You suggested someone who knows about killing, and how the police work a crime scene. I said, maybe it was a cop. Fits the profile of what you were saying."

"Or someone who studied crime."

"Lester, do you think it could be as simple as that?"

"What do you mean, Louise?"

"A cop, an emergency ambulance attendant, a doctor, a nurse, a—"

"A crime scene technician," Lester blurted, interrupting Louise. "Whoever cased the joint knew schedules of the housekeeper, the pool service, and the gardener."

"Yes, Lester, any of them," she said, sashaying back to her desk.

"Get me Lieutenant Walker."

"Right away."

"Ron, it's Lester. Meet me at the Bimini Lounge inside the Colony Hotel at 6 pm. I've got to run this by you-in person."

"Jesus H Christ, Caine. You choose the most expensive places in town. You better be buying."

Lester could never figure out or ask people why they used that expression—'Jesus H Christ.' Christ never used a middle initial.

The Colony Hotel, a harbor for the well-heeled, dressed to impress. This exclusive address beckoned state leaders, movie stars, presidents and the 'nose-in-the-air-shits,' Lester coldly called the wealthy snobs, excluding The Duke and Duchess of Windsor who were frequent guests.

Six on the dot, Walker approached Lester who was already nursing a drink at the bar while lounge singer, Savana Rose, seductively soothed the hearts of those floundering in misery, as happens occasionally with Lester. Ron's drink was ready like a lonely lover waiting for a pickup line... *Do you come here often?*

Their discussion was an eye opener for Ron, who hadn't given Lester's theory a tumble...until now.

"Lester, what you're laying out to me is so bizarre. There are a lot of probabilities. It's incredible. No matter how long I've been on the job or how long I know you, I keep learning from you. I should be grateful, but it pisses me off." Ron tapped his glass twice on the bar for a refill. "There are probably dozens of family members of victims that we don't know about, as you said, and we don't have a clue how many want vengeance. I know what's going to take place, and so do you."

"Someone has to spend days in the Miami office of Vanderbilt, Harper and St. James going through their archives. There's no way around it. He was an important person—a judge. I still have some angles to work. Was anything removed from the scene I should know about?

"No! There wasn't anything my men came across out of the ordinary. I would have told you."

Bullshit! Trumpeted in Lester's ear. He knew cops and cops only share what's to their benefit. Somehow, though, Lester felt Lieutenant Walker was telling the truth, unlike the envelope he found taped to the bottom of Desmond's night table drawer. *What the hell was Libby asking about then? Did she know about the envelope and what it contains? What was Desmond in to? Was Libby or H-2 part of whatever Desmond was hiding from Lorraine? She knows something. Now, I've got to contend with Libby, Lorraine, Walker and the envelope.*

CHAPTER 20

1932 to 1943.

Vanderbilt, Harper and St. James's law firm buzzed with activity, clients, and major national headlines. They never expected a little over a decade ago so many trials would fall into their laps so soon after the Archdiocese murder case involving Father Fairchild and his lover, Cynthia Beall. That steamy lovers' trial grabbed national headlines.

The three partners knew the importance of courtroom demeanor and how it could sway those passing judgment—the jury, and the official in charge— the judge. Cool competency influenced the judge's decisions when the prosecutor objected, reducing their risk of being overruled. They honed their craft like actors for the silver screen, which won them national acclaim. It also attracted members of victims' families who might want revenge on Desmond, Libby, and H-2 for their successful verdicts.

Clients from all over Florida flocked to their office leading to one trial after another. Additional attorneys, legal assistants and office staff required adding more office area to keep up with the demand. Their practice became a revolving door—burn 'em and turn 'em. Their bank accounts grew by the day.

World War II was beginning in 1939, when Nazi Germany, under Adolf Hitler, invaded Poland. This assault started a war that raged through 1945, involving most of the world's countries, including the great powers, and led to the formation of two opposing military alliances.

In December 1941, the United States entered the war.

Desmond, Libby, and H-2 with Judges Dasby Warner and Harris Bleakly saw the writing on the wall way before the call of duty to help their mother country. They formed a munitions factory that produced bullets for the war effort. This move exempted them from military service with a II-B deferment. Much of their munitions supplied the Naval Amphibious Training Base 128 miles north in Ft. Pierce, where 50,000 troops trained for the Normandy invasion.

Their part of the war effort not only made them wealthy, but supported their research and financed an interest group to investigate war crimes. Who better? They were in the business of crime, after all.

By the time the war ended, over 100 million people from over thirty countries were affected. Oceans of blood soaked into the earth's soil.

CHAPTER 21

1868 Wilshire Court,

The home of Lorraine Vanderbilt

and the scene of Judge Vanderbilt's murder.

L ester set out to find some needed answers and direction from Lorraine at her home. He knew Libby would not be around until later in the day and the housekeeper was off. Lorraine was literally in her own jail—not allowed to leave town. She withdrew to the same room where she found Desmond's body, although cleaned by a company specializing in cleaning crime scenes. Visitors would never realize a murder took place there. An outsider would consider this property an oasis in paradise.

Lester's 1948 Cadillac Series 62 Convertible turned into the circular driveway. The top down and the high gloss shine of the special Caddy Horizon Blue exterior paint with Deep Blue leather interior turned the heads of neighbors who were dog walking or gawking at 1868 Wilshire Court. Lester cordially waved, smiling, proud of his automobile and the stature it gave him.

The doorbell played eight notes. Its melodic chime should have been a welcome sound—someone bringing warmth for the spirit. Instead, the eight notes announced a deliberate coldness of a soul gone bad. No answer. Lester pushed the button with a small light beside it that urged the caller to *do it again.* He did. Still no answer.

Lester strolled the stone pathway leading to the back of the house, opening his suit jacket, and placing his palm over the butt of his .38 revolver, not knowing what he would find. He gazed through each window he passed until he reached the backyard.

Lorraine sunbathed on the pool deck, reading as she loved to do. A cigarette dangled from her cherry red lips, a vodka martini next to her at the ready. It was 10 am. Lester stopped, took a deep breath, and admired this beautiful woman, seeing why Desmond had said lightning hit him when he saw her on stage. Here on her lounge, her naked body was still magnificent at age fifty.

"Lorraine," he called. "Lorraine," he repeated louder when he received no response.

"Jesus Christ, Lester. You scared me. Is it that time already?" Lorraine sat up.

Lester regarded her nakedness while she gathered herself. He strolled over and picked up her robe from the concrete floor of the pool deck.

"Better put this on," and he held it for her as he glanced at the title of the book she was reading. Smiling, he thought how appropriate—*The Naked and the Dead* by Norman Mailer.

"You are always a gentleman. Your Mama taught you well." She slipped into it, giving him a smile of thanks. "Would you like a drink?"

"Sure, I had my coffee." Lester grimaced, uncomfortable with her remark about his mother. *She doesn't know her.*

"Let's go inside. You get comfy while I dress. Make yourself a drink. The bar is in the dining room. I won't be long. Make me a fresh one while you're at it."

Lester located the bar and poured himself a bourbon, neat, and lit up a smoke, first tapping it on his lighter as usual. He was relaxed, only caring for frills in certain things at certain times and with certain company.

He let his mind roam over Lorraine as he'd seen her on the lounge—her smooth, delightful skin; those long dancer's legs; her angel eyes longing for him; her perky, perfect breasts. His body tightened as he imagined his tongue circling her pink nipples, so pink they matched the roses in her garden. He could almost feel her sunset auburn hair cascading over her shoulders on to his chest.

"Lester!" He heard Lorraine say his name in a stronger than usual voice, shaking him from his daytime wonderland about night things.

"Come down to earth. Bring your drink. I enjoy sitting by the pool and listening to the waterfalls. It gives me solace. Lester, I'm worried—"

"I can have Lieutenant Walker bring back a babysitter for you. Station a car in your driveway with around the clock officers."

"No! But thank you. If someone's going to get me, they will, no matter where I am or who's with me. I don't go out these days because Lieutenant Walker told me to stay put. Rosemary is great. She does all the housekeeping, shopping, gets the mail at the post office, picks up the laundry. I don't know what I'd do without her, but I need to get out. I don't believe whoever killed Desmond...." She paused, expression bleak and tears streaking her mascara.

Lester handed her his pocket square handkerchief.

"C'mon," he said. "Libby won't be here for hours. Let's get a late breakfast at *Testa's*. The chef makes the best eggs Benedict in Palm Beach." Lester took Lorraine's hand, helping her stand, bringing them nose to nose. He removed the hankie she was holding and wiped her cheeks.

Lester broke the long silence and stare. "Go freshen up. Meet me in the car."

Locals crowded *Testa's*, although some tourists checked out its reputation. Lester and Lorraine sat outside, enjoying the sea breeze that rolled in from the sandy beach a stone's throw from where they sat. The indistinct chatter and laughter from the other patrons was a welcome song to Lorraine.

"Ah, good morning, Mr. Caine, Ma'am. So good to see you. Shall I get you both coffee?" handing them menus.

"Thank you, Joe. No menus. We'll have the eggs Benedict, two black coffees, and two Bloody Marys. Hold the celery and substitute another shot of vodka."

"Yes, sir, Mr. Caine. Comin' right up." Joe did extras for Lester, knowing he would show his appreciation with a hefty tip.

"Okay, Lorraine. Tell me why you don't think you have to worry about being killed. What do you know about anyone who came to the house or what Desmond may have been involved in? Did Desmond conduct private meetings at the house?"

"Never, Lester," she answered with conviction. "All the company we had, we both knew. Desmond rarely spoke about the trials or criminals he sentenced, even the cases when he sentenced them to the electric chair."

"I went to one execution with 'Old Sparky'," Joe interrupted, bringing their coffee and Bloody Marys. The waiter interrupted Lester's questions. He stared at his Bloody Mary, shook out two cigarettes and tapped the ends on his cigarette lighter to keep the tobacco firm, a habit from his Navy days, before lighting them. He handed one to Lorraine.

"Lester, the Medical Examiner will release Desmond in a few days. Will you help me with the funeral arrangements?"

"Of course, Lorraine. I thought Libby was helping you, but no matter. I'll be by your side. Whatever you need, I will be there for you."

"I knew you would. I just had to hear you say it. You're a good man, Lester."

"Tell that to my ex-wives, Lorraine," he said to lighten up. "You said a few times that you are scared and that looks can be deceiving. Care to explain?"

"I fear not knowing what and who Desmond may have been involved with. I told you, he had paid back all the favors to those individuals who helped him reach his judge's chair and his eventual position politically. Maybe one of those unsavory persons did this. It could also be a vengeful family member or friend of someone Desmond got off when he was a defense attorney. Maybe it's a family member seeking retribution for not getting it in the court. That's what Libby said."

"I don't know, Lester. I'm confused. Desmond defended a lot of thugs and helped them walk away from their crimes clean. There were some from the Cleopatra and some that frequented Palm Island. You know exactly who I'm talking about. And yet, Desmond had a heart of gold. He set up a few widows with pensions in trusts with the banks. Their money didn't last forever, the depression and all. Many banks failed and so did the widows' pensions. They were penniless. Desmond arranged that the law firm would continue to pay the widows until they died, even if something happened to him. He used his own money, Lester. Desmond was a good man."

"I never knew that about Desmond. It makes me wonder. I understand your concerns. Libby, H-2, me, the Palm Beach Police, and the Miami police are looking into past cases that Desmond tried, just because of what you said. Many people hated him and Libby and H-2 for defending those lawbreakers on the road to Perdition. Those they defended, their behavior and life failures were evil. Here lies the grind. Who did the dirty deed? Someone who was not happy Desmond stopped repaying favors, or a victim's family member who felt the perpetrator got off too light or was found not guilty. None of those criminals ever acted with compassion or imitated the *Good Samaritan*. Many people feel they deserved to die, like someone felt about Desmond. Who knows? Maybe Libby or H-2 are next."

"I know, Lester. But there are too many files, too many people, probably hundreds over the years. It will take weeks, maybe months, to go through all the files. What was he involved in and with who? That's what I fear. I don't want to know, and yet I do. I can't think about it anymore today. Let's just talk. Lester, you know me better than I know you just from my past. Why don't you tell me about..." her voice died away.

"About?" Lester questioned.

"Well, I don't want to pry. You know what? Yes, I do. Your whole countenance changed back at the house when I mentioned your mama and how she taught you well. Is she still with us?"

"Oh, yes," he answered, his tone sharp.

Lorraine watched his handsome face tighten. Hazel eyes, chiseled jaw with cleft chin. Just showing gray at his temples. His hair a little long, just this side of shaggy, in step with the trumpet player she remembered who loved jazz.

"Pamela lives in Lake Worth for the past few years. She's seventy-one. That's one reason I came here among others." Lester sighed. "She abandoned me for the first two months of my life. My mother left me in the hospital." He swallowed hard.

"Oh, my god, why?" Lorraine exclaimed, turning heads from nearby tables.

Lester leaned toward Lorraine, motioning for her to keep it down.

"My father was a gambler and disappeared for days at a time. He wasn't there when it was time for my mother to give birth to me. He was shot and killed in a back-alley dice game. My mother faced this alone and took care of my brother, Francis, three years older than me. She never bonded with me the way she did with him, maybe because of all those years with my brother before I was born, or maybe because she had another mouth to feed and no husband."

"He was special to her. He was a breech baby and she went through a difficult birth almost losing him, and she almost died. He was born on St. Patrick's Day and got Patrick as his middle name. My mother said he would have the luck of the Irish. I always said he was born with his head up his ass."

"Anyway, Francis was her favorite and got all the attention. You know, music, dancing, acting lessons. He was going to Hollywood; she was going to see to it. Come Halloween, Pamela dressed me up like a girl and Francis as a pirate. I ripped all those photos out of the family album. She won't miss them with all the other photos of Francis she has on display. Anyway, you get the picture."

"Where is Francis now?"

"He's dead, and my mother grieves for him every day as a mother should. She filled her apartment with pictures from the talent shows where he performed. It's not natural for a parent to bury their children. I hate to go there, always reminded of her love for him over me, but she's my mother. I have to be sure she's eating, getting to the doctor, and checking in with her friends. They look out for one another."

"Lorraine, I've never told anyone, but she treated me the way no son should be treated. It still influences me, forty-eight years later. Maybe it's why I never stayed married or had kids. I'm sorry, I didn't mean to bore you." Lester looked away to hide his embarrassment.

Lorraine's eyes welled up, and she covered Lester's hand.

"It's okay, Lorraine. I've accepted it. I feel guilty that I don't feel for my mother the way a son should. But she's my mother and I have to see that she's okay."

"Lester, I've always said it. You are a good, no, a great man. You should be proud of yourself. Would you like me to come with you? I will. We'll visit Pamela. I'd love to meet her."

"Maybe, but not today. Today is about you."

CHAPTER 22

Clematis Street.

Roslyn Wanamaker impatiently waited for Lester to arrive at Lester Caine Investigations. She had arrived shortly after Louise opened the office and sat tapping her fingers on the arm of her chair.

"Mrs. Wanamaker, Lester will be here soon. Would you like coffee and a donut while you wait?" Louise's slight southern drawl dripped a sweetness she didn't feel.

"Coffee would be fine, thank you."

Lester opened the door, and Roslyn rose to her feet, surprising him.

"Mr. Caine, someone is following me, trying to kill me. Please Mr. Caine, help me." Lester shot a puzzled glance at Louise, raising an eyebrow. *What the hell is she doing here and what is she talking about?*

Louise shrugged.

"Mrs. Wanamaker, come inside. I see you're upset. Let's talk over coffee."

"Mr. Caine, I want some sort of protection. I'm being followed. Maybe I'll be killed."

"Mrs. Wanamaker, I know you are being followed. I put a tail on you. It's one of my people. I should have let you know. It's for your own good. I'm having you followed for your protection. I apologize for upsetting you. Let me make it up to you. I'll take us to lunch. How does that sound?" He gave her a full wattage smile designed to pacify her.

"Well, Mr. Caine, that sounds very nice, but we would have to go where no one would recognize me."

"Of course. We'll go to Hialeah Park."

"The racetrack?" she asked with a dubious twist to her lips.

"Yes. Have you ever been to the races?"

"Well, no, I haven't. It could be fun, I guess." She glanced away, unenthusiastic.

Lester paused to speak to Louise while Roslyn continued to the elevator. He whispered, "Call Gloria. Have her meet us at Hialeah."

"Good luck," Louise called.

Any day the ponies were running was a great day at Hialeah. The flamingos, a famous trademark of the park, soared over the infield to the strains of *Flamingo*[10],

---

[10] "Flamingo" (1940) is a popular song and jazz standard written by Ted Grouya with lyrics by Edmund Anderson and first recorded

116

putting on a show before landing on the infield lake. The world elite, decked out in suits and elaborate hats, clamored beside a dirt track, anxiously awaiting the signal for the thoroughbreds to race around the oval. Habitues of the Park often called the horses *ponies,* although they weighed upward of nine hundred pounds. You never knew who you would see at Hialeah— celebrities from stage and screen, political figures, and often Scarface, Al Capone himself with his henchmen. The city officials, police from the top brass down, and local politicians were on the dole and looked the other way.

Lester knew exactly where to find Scarecrow. This time she had two seats saved for her arriving guests.

"Lester, here," Gloria said, giving a wave.

"Oh, my god! Mr. Caine, it's her. She's the one following me! Do something. Shoot her!" Roslyn shrilled, turning heads.

"Mrs. Wanamaker, please calm down. This is Gloria Saville. She's a private investigator who works with me. She's following you for your protection."

"My God! I've been having nightmares the past few nights thinking I'm going to be killed."

"Mrs. Wanamaker, sit. I'm protecting you," Gloria said. "If I were the person hired to kill you, I could have done it many times. I must tell you for your own good,

---

by singer Herb Jeffries and the Duke Ellington Orchestra on December 28, 1940, for Victor Records.

stop going to Burdines to see Millie Sparks. If she suspects you, your goose is cooked. We want to implicate her as well as Mr. Wanamaker and the hired gun. We're very close to sorting this out. Please listen and follow our direction. Now, let's enjoy the ponies. Have you ever been here?"

"Well, no. And I must admit I'm quite impressed. I thought—"

"This place was for degenerate gamblers? A place for the down and out trying to score big?" Gloria answered with a knowing smile.

"I...yes, I'm ashamed to say. These could be my neighbors or from the Country Club. I... I'm embarrassed. I never knew. How does this work?" she asked, showing interest.

"Simple. You select a horse and place your bet for the horse to win or for the horse to place, which means you think he'll come in first or second. Or, if you want to play it safer, you wager the horse will show. That way you receive a payoff if the horse finishes first, second or third. If you learn to handicap, you'll study the racing form to determine the horse's ability, its jockey's record and experience. You'll read the tote board to see what odds the horse is paying. Some people buy a tout sheet. For now, pick a horse you like."

"I like this horse's name, *Lola's Always Right*. A woman, Mr. Caine, is always right. Isn't that correct, Miss Saville?"

"You bet, Mrs. Wanamaker. C'mon, follow me to the betting window. Have some cash ready." Gloria leaned close to Lester as she passed. "We need to talk. I can't believe what I found from tailing her."

"Oh Miss. Saville, what do you want me to do?" Roslyn asked, interrupting Gloria like a child, waiting for instructions.

"I'm coming, Mrs. Wanamaker."

"Gloria, don't tell me you're slipping in your old age. Roslyn spotted you," Lester teased, smiling widely, showing his full set of choppers.

"Fuck you, Lester," Gloria whispered. "She's complicated, has a lot of friends, and goes a lot of places." On the field, jockeys in colorful silks clasped their horse's reins. Horses raised their heads, ready for business as the *Call to the Post* played. Outriders ponied them around the track to the starting gate, trying to calm the thoroughbreds and keep their focus on the race.

Snorts and an occasional whinny pierced the air as horse and rider entered the cages. The slam of the rear doors sent a wave of sound through the crowd, adding to the horses' anxiety. Some horses balked at entering the starting gate and had to be led into the barrier.

Once settled, the bell rang, and the gates opened. The announcer said, "And they're off," to the cheers of the crowd. The pounding hooves thundered, and the announcer called each horse's position on the track. Roslyn leaped to her feet, urging *Lola's Always Right* to victory like she was a seasoned pro. The jockeys crouched over their horse's neck, riding to win. The horses seemed to float in the air, graceful as a ballerina, for a span clocked in minutes.

"Now what?" Roslyn asked after the race was over. Her eyes sparkled and her cheeks were flushed. "Can we do another?"

"Sure can. Your horse didn't pay anything. It came in fourth place. No payout. We can do one more before we head to the lounge," Gloria said.

"Yes, let's do another. They have a bar here too?" Roslyn asked.

"And entertainment." Gloria said, luring her into becoming a racing fan.

Approaching the Mediterranean lounge, they heard the music of the Sonny Abbott Trio.

As soon as they placed their drinks order, Gloria told Roslyn, "I know for sure no one is following you, so I am going to stop tailing you. You can go about your daily activities–The Club and Spa, your errands, and doctors. Stay away from Burdines. Shop at Macy's or Saks."

Roslyn stared at Gloria, raising one eyebrow as if to say, *are you fucking kidding me, sister.*

"We know who Mr. Wanamaker is working with. Don't worry, Mrs. Wanamaker. You'll be safe. Just follow our directions. Now, I want you to have a dinner party and invite me as a dinner guest to meet your husband. Set it up with a few other guests and encourage your husband to include his poker buddies as an excuse to meet his friends. Make him believe you're taking an interest in what he likes. And do it soon."

"I will, Miss Saville. I can make that happen."

"Mr. Caine, will you see me home when we get to my car?"

"Yes, of course, Mrs. Wanamaker."

"Roslyn, Mr. Caine. You can call me Roslyn."

"And Roslyn, we need to call each other by our first names," Gloria said. "Remember, I'm your friend. And when you introduce me to the dinner party, I'll be Gloria Parrish. You can remember that, can't you?"

"Of course, Gloria. Gloria Parrish."

CHAPTER 23

Memorial Service for Judge Vanderbilt.

The ME released Desmond's body to the Royal Palm Memorial Gardens, where Lorraine and Lester had planned Desmond's memorial service. Following the memorial service, he would be interred at West Palm Beach Woodlawn Cemetery.

Lorraine wanted a modest service, not the standing room only event that overflowed the Chapel. But how could there be anything else with Desmond, Libby, and H-2's law practice involved with hundreds of people over so many years—politicians, police, gangsters, murderers, thieves, real estate developers, lawyers, judges, men of the cloth, high-ranking military advisors with the munitions factory, and the movers and shakers of Miami, Florida. They came to pay their respects to Desmond, but Lieutenant Ron Walker and his men attended for a different reason—scoping out everyone and snapping candid photos of anyone they thought could be a suspect. More times than not, suspects were in the forefront of investigations, even volunteering, so they could see how the case was progressing. The police knew this.

The room fell silent with the toll of the chapel's bell, a slow rhythmic cadence reminiscent of the passage in *The Hunchback of Notre Dame*—Quasimodo ringing the large bell he called Mary, the one he liked best. At its silence, the altar boy rang The Chimes of the Trinity three times, representing the Father, Son, and Holy Spirit.

Everyone rose to witness His Excellency, Monsignor O'Malley, process down the aisle behind an altar boy bearing the cross aloft. He genuflected in front of the Christ. Light murmuring from some of the assembly recalled the Monsignor had paid a lot of money to Desmond's firm to get the priest and his lover acquitted of murder.

Monsignor O'Malley turned to the crowd, made the sign of the cross and recited a blessing before proceeding to Desmond's bier. The wreath of flowers beside it filled the air with a sweet perfume. The cleric lay his hands upon the coffin, bowed, and kissed it before returning to the pulpit. All sat in unison.

"I am heartbroken by the tragic death of my friend and Christian brother, whose life was prematurely ended by violence, by murder."

Gasps punctuated his unexpected words, unusual from a holy man. Lorraine tightened her grip on Lester's hand as his other hand did to Gloria's and hers to Louise.

"Desmond Vanderbilt lies in the bosom of our Lord and Savior, Jesus Christ. Nowhere is there a safer or more peaceful place," the Monsignor said. "I am honored to have known Desmond, and urge you to share your emotions, your memories, that they may comfort loved ones and friends Desmond left behind, not only on this day, but for the days, weeks, months and years that are ahead."

He looked at Lorraine and continued. "His lovely wife, Lorraine, was his counterpart—strong, intelligent, loving, and kind. My dear, this is not goodbye." He swept the sea of mourners with his hand. "To his many friends, associates, and relatives, this is a celebration of Desmond's life, a life that brought joy and happiness to many. His influence will continue for years to come."

"Let us remember the words of our dear Psalmist, David: *The Lord is my shepherd; I shall not want. He maketh me to lie down in green pastures; He leadeth me beside the still waters. He restoreth my soul; He leadeth me in the paths of righteousness for His name's sake. Yea, though I walk through the valley of the shadow of death, I will fear no evil for thou art with me; thy rod and thy staff comfort me.* Dear God, Holy Father, you are the source of love and comfort. Keep us in life and in death in your abiding love, and, by your grace, lead us to your kingdom. Lord, shine your face upon Desmond and be gracious to our dearly departed, so he may be at eternal peace. This I pray through your Son, and our Savior, Jesus Christ. Amen."

"Amen!" softly echoed in the chapel. The altar boy handed Monsignor O'Malley the Gold Thurible on a long gold chain. He walked around Desmond's coffin gently swinging it, releasing the sweet-smelling smoke of the incense, symbolizing the soul of the deceased ascending to Heaven.

"Desmond must be rolling over in that box," Lorraine whispered to Lester. "He could not and would not subject himself to all this ceremony he considered nonsensical. I'm sure he's waiting to hear who's going to say what about him."

I'd rather he sit up and point to his murderer. That would be a damn sight more helpful than rolling around. Lester quickly followed his smart ass thought with *Sorry, Lord.*

Lorraine knew there would be a sincere outpouring from hearts who loved Desmond and those who owed him. And then there would be lies and bullshit from people who came to keep up appearances, saying what was expected, that they really didn't mean.

The eulogies took two hours. Lorraine had to be strong, like Desmond would have wanted. It seemed everyone had a Desmond story they wanted to share. There were stories that brought tears, smiles, and hearty laughter.

Lorraine knew what she was about to face, and she dreaded facing it alone. What was Desmond's involvement and with whom? What was it that got him killed?

CHAPTER 24

Miami

The home of Dr. Wayne and Roslyn Wanamaker.

Roslyn set up the dinner party as instructed by Gloria. She and her husband hosted the group: Van Kudos, the top ophthalmologist in his field who performed delicate eye surgeries from war injuries, accidents and birth defects, accompanied by his wife, Gina; Roslyn's mother, Mildred; and Mr. and Mrs. Jean-Paul Laurent, the Miami mercenary who ran the guns for hire. Wayne Wanamaker and Jean-Paul had become friends, closer than needed to kill Roslyn. If Roslyn had followed their plan, it was a sure bet, better than the odds at Hialeah, that she'd meet Mr. Laurent.

Cocktails were served pool side, the setting reminiscent of a scene in James A. Michener's *South Pacific*[11]. Soft breezes whispering exotic nothings passed over the guests. Introductions were early on as the cocktails flowed before the dinner bell chimed. If

---

[11] A scene in Michener's Pulitzer Prize winning collection of sequentially related stories set in the South Pacific during World War II.

Roslyn knew who Jean-Paul really was, she would be hysterical. *We would have to call an ambulance and put her in a straitjacket,* Gloria thought. She would keep a close eye on Roslyn. *Maybe that would be an easier way to get rid of her than murder.* Gloria's thoughts were getting out of control, the closer she got to Roslyn, but she was delighted Roslyn had followed her instructions, cozying up to her husband to invite a poker buddy. Gloria had known the Doc would invite Jean-Paul and not any of the other *shleps*, as Roslyn called them. In her snobbery, she viewed them as commoners.

The Wanamaker's always hired extra servers their housekeeper oversaw. They set the dinner table to perfection suitable for a Royal Family—embroidered linen napkins so soft they could diaper a baby, fine China, and monogrammed silverware that gleamed in the light emanating from the dining room chandelier.

Gloria was a smooth operator using her skills from the Summer Stock Playhouse theater and her special operations military training. She wasn't shy and participated in conversation, keeping it simple. "Isn't the weather spectacular?" to local politics, medical news, war efforts, investments, and sex or lives of shallow Hollywood stars, in her opinion.

Roslyn introduced Gloria as a member of her Bridge Club. No one was the wiser since Wayne never interfered with Roslyn's activities, just as she didn't interfere with his poker games.

"Tell me, Ms. Parrish, what is it you do?" Jean-Paul asked, separating himself and Gloria from the incoherent jibber-jabber of the other guests.

"Please, Mr. Laurent, we don't have to be formal, do we? You can call me Gloria and I'll address you as Jean-Paul, if you're okay with that." She smiled, plotting for him to lower the barrier. Parrish was a name Gloria used as an alias, to be sure nothing would appear if he did a background check on her. Knowing the business Jean-Paul was in, he would vet her if he lived up to his reputation.

"Of course, Gloria. Tell me, what is it you do exactly?" Jean-Paul asked again.

This is like winning The Irish Sweepstakes[12], Gloria thought, prematurely reveling in her success.

"I'm in the second-hand wholesale business, Jean-Paul. I sell anything I can to anyone who has the cash."

"That's quite interesting, Gloria. I supply and sell wholesale as well. I sell to some, shall we say, just as you, who want certain items for a price." Jean-Paul slyly answered like an investigative reporter baiting his subject. "I have great clients overseas. One of my best sellers is a hard-to-find item—patent leather boots."

"Patent leather boots?" Gloria questioned. "Who wants patent leather Boots?

Jean-Paul's hearty laugh rang out. "The Far Eastern Desert Army. Who would have ever thought in a

---

[12] The Irish Sweepstakes is touted to be a good cause. It lends support to the hospitals in Ireland. Although it is illegal in the US, millions of tickets are sold each year.

million years that soldiers in the desert would want their boots to be patent leather?"

"Maybe we could do some business together," Gloria said. "That just may fit something I can help you with in the future. I'm pretty solid at the moment with my clients. I maneuver heavy duty merchandise and don't know if yours will fit with mine. One never knows. Tell me, what is it you push?"

"I, too, am into hard-to-get merchandise like the boots. I also deal in many other *heavy* items. Why don't we set up a time to meet? Now, let's enjoy and join the flow of the conversations."

"That would be nice, Jean-Paul. I look forward to it. Somehow, I'm feeling a good collaboration."

"If we do meet again, why, we shall smile; if not, why, then this parting was well made.[13]" Jean-Paul replied, handing Gloria his business card, the same one Roslyn came across.

Mercenaries and Guns for Hire

Leave First Name & Telephone Number Only

MI 5-1500

"A well-read man who quotes Shakespeare," Gloria said, as she looked without expression at what he handed her. "We may be able to do more together than sell boots in the desert." Gloria raised her wineglass. "Cheers."

"Cheers," he said."

---

[13] William Shakespeare

CHAPTER 25

West Flagler Street, Miami,

Law offices of Vanderbilt, Harper and St. James

Lieutenant Walker and Lester were out of leads. Libby and H-2 agreed they had to review the files in storage. VH&S rented space in a remote area in the Courthouse basement and stored their archived files there. Libby and H-2 rarely visited the dusty, poorly ventilated area. That's what paralegals and clerks were for. The lighting took forever to come on, flickering in a surreal show that was not only annoying but hard on the eyes.

The stale smell of old conflicts filled the investigators' noses, followed by throat clearing and sneezing. This massive task was a product of the evil that had brought them all together. Two hundred sixty voluminous case files spanned thirteen years from the firm's establishment until Desmond became a Judge. Their law firm had been so sought after, they only handled high-profile cases that generated huge fees. Desmond, Libby and H-2 hadn't expected the flood of work so soon on the coattails of *State of Florida vs. Timothy Fairchild and Cynthia Beall*, which case had been supported by the Archdiocese.

Many of their high-profile cases were with the likes of Lorenzo Lentini and Laurel Hennessey and grabbed national headlines.

LOVER'S THREESOME HOTTER THAN THE MIAMI SUN.

MURDER OR SUICIDE

Lorenzo Lentini, a sixty-two-year-old pilot, and his much younger British wife by two decades, Laurel Hennessey, were down on their luck and almost destitute of life's necessities in Miami. Captain Lentini's glory days as an Italian fighter pilot and war hero were long gone, and the Italian airline where he had flown commercially forced him to retire.

The war was over. Lorenzo and Laurel faced a different battle—survival. No money, no prestige, no glory. They searched desperately for the life they once knew. Alcohol became their refuge. They met Adam Belmont at a local bar known for heavy drinking and promiscuousness. Mr. Belmont claimed to be a writer and a decent one, with one published book.

Laurel convinced Lorenzo to invite Adam to move in with them in their Coconut Grove home. They had a spare bedroom to offer him. Laurel thought Adam would fit in with the Grove's distinct Bohemian flair of artists, intellectuals and adventurers like Lorenzo and Laurel. Their offer began on a professional level. Belmont would ghost write Lorenzo's life story as a highly decorated war hero. Who knew? Maybe the published book would be a bestseller, and they'd get a movie contract.

Laurel and Lorenzo believed they had an *open* marriage. Laurel kept her maiden name and agreed to a *ménage à trois*.[14] But Laurel fell in love with Adam, a captivating lover. Lorenzo walked in unexpectedly, surprising the lovers in the thick of passion. This was not what Lorenzo and Laurel had agreed upon—sex with a third person only if both of them were present and took part. In a jealous rage, Lorenzo shot Adam in the head, presenting it as a suicide. Even with the suicide note in Belmont's typewriter, the cops arrested Lorenzo Lentini and charged him with Adam's murder.

This made steamy headlines, and the trial packed the courtroom daily. Photographers' flash bulbs exploded, momentarily blinding spectators or filling their vision with spots.

Laurel Hennessey took the stand and swore to tell the truth, the whole truth.... Reporters dashed off scribbled notes for their editors, hoping their coverage of this trial would win them the American Journalist Award for reporting.

The prosecutor bullied, badgered, and verbally bludgeoned Laurel to admit the murder stemmed from their debauched lifestyle. Like bullets fired in fast succession from a Thompson submachine gun ala gangster *Machine Gun Kelly,* his raised voice, harsh tactics, finger pointing, and accusations did not win points with the jury.

---

[14] Menage-a-trois is French for threesome

Vanderbilt, Harper and St. James stood their ground, letting the prosecution persecute Laurel until she sobbed, uncontrollable. Libby St. James acted as lead defense attorney. Desmond conducted the cross-examination.

Libby had warned Laurel not to cave even when the judge asked if she was okay or needed a break. "Press on," Libby advised. She coached Laurel to convince the jury that although she had loved Adam, Laurel realized Lorenzo was her genuine love. She knew he had an undying love for her. Their alcohol and sexual appetites made her the cause of Adam's death, not Lorenzo's jealousy.

Desmond found a forensic expert who testified Adam committed suicide and the suicide note was real. Libby persuaded the jury that Laurel's genuine commitment to Lorenzo caused Adam's suicide. The jury sympathized with Laurel, despite her lifestyle; hated the prosecutor for his behavior; and found Lorenzo not guilty.

Because of the trial's publicity, Lorenzo received backing to fly around the world, trying to break the current record. Lorenzo's plane with him and Laurel aboard disappeared and was never found. The newspapers eulogized the duo as a modern-day Romeo and Juliet.

Case after case rolled in. VHS expanded their offices, added more attorneys, and occupied the entire fifth floor. Their payday was huge.

The junior attorneys handled hundreds of misdemeanor cases each year, the bread-and-butter work. Desmond, Libby and H-2 didn't even consider them.

Interns shlepped the two-hundred and sixty cartons of mice chewed boxes to the fifth-floor office, stacking them against the wall in a conference room. Files covered the large mahogany table and were strewn on the floor.

"Jesus H Christ! These boxes have mice shit in them," Walker said, coughing and sneezing from the odor emanating from the files. "Whose fucking idea was this, anyway? Never mind, it was mine," he mumbled into his handkerchief.

CHAPTER 26

Miami,

Burdines Department Store.

Gloria's years of training in the military and law enforcement and her life experience told her Roslyn would not sit on her hands. Roslyn had been belligerent when Gloria suggested she stop stalking Millie. Gloria knew it had thrown Roslyn into a tizzy. Her eyes had reflected a distant stare of shark eyes.

Gloria made her way to the second-floor men's department, spotting Millie ringing out a customer. Then she headed to the dressing room to pick up any clothes left behind. *Goddamn it! I knew it! That fucking Roslyn didn't listen.*

Roslyn loitered in plain view. Without hesitation, when Millie went to the dressing room, Roslyn made her move. Her expensive heels clicked rhythmically across the highly polished tile floor.

Gloria intercepted her. "What the fuck is wrong with you, Roslyn? I should arrest you. I can do that, you know. You can't fuck this up. You want your husband to pay, don't you?"

"I want him to pay until it hurts, *and* this bitch too."

"They will, but only if you stop this madness. Otherwise, it's you that will spend the rest of your life in prison. Now give me the gun," Gloria said, holding out her hand.

"How do you know I have a gun?" Roslyn asked, visibly shaken.

"Because it's in your hand. Now give it over, nice and easy. I'm not even going to ask where you got it. But if you pull a stunt like this again, *Lester Caine Investigations* will drop you, and you'll be the one behind bars. I'll see to it. Do I make myself clear?"

"It won't happen again. I promise. I have to find a restroom. I think I peed my panties."

CHAPTER 27

O^h shit! Lester, we have to stop meeting like this," Gloria burst into laughter, spooning her naked body against his back.

"Good morning, Gloria," reaching to pat her butt. "Be a good girl and put up some coffee while I start the shower."

"Lester, I have a surprise for you. I'll tell you when we have our coffee," Gloria said with a lilt in her voice. "You'll like this."

"I can't wait," Lester said, a touch of irony in his voice as he threw the covers to the side. *Shit! I hope she's not pregnant.*

Gloria poured the coffee, Lester's black and strong. She dawdled over her cup of Joe, pouring cream, and slowly stirring the hot liquid to melt the two sugar cubes she dropped into the cup. She took a sip, slurping, smiling at Lester like a kid who'd discovered candy on his pillow, building the suspense just like she knew how to do in bed.

"Are you ready, Detective? I have a surprise for you."

"Gloria, I was born ready and I love your surprises."

"Yes, I know, and you like my surprises. But you may not be ready for this one."

Please don't be pregnant. Lester straightened, preparing himself, like a kid on Christmas morning who didn't see the bike he'd asked for.

"Okay, c'mon, tell me. What? I've been patiently waiting."

The phone rang, interrupting Gloria.

"Damn!" Lester said.

"You better answer it," Gloria said. "You never know who's on the other end of the receiver. It could be Governor Caldwell wanting to give you a Humanitarian Award." She burst into laughter, appreciating her wit.

Lester made a face and took the receiver. "Hello?... Mom. Okay, okay. Slow down. I'll be there shortly."

Pamela lived in Lake Worth only nine miles away as the crow flies. With traffic, it took him eighteen minutes, not rushing to a crime scene or dodging pedestrians and the steel columns of the El Train as he used to do in his unmarked police cruiser through New York City streets. Although there had been panic in Pamela's voice, Lester knew her claim that someone was trying to get into her apartment was false. That was her way of getting him to visit. As usual, it turned out to be nothing. It further annoyed him because he knew his brother Francis would have ignored her.

Lester always accommodated Pamela. He knew her paranoia—the combination of drinking and meds—would and could cause her panic. He couldn't recount the number of times he had encouraged her to become a friend of "Bill," or wear the "White Ribbon."[15]

"Lester, you're a good boy. Always there for me. Please check the windows and doors. Your favorite chocolate is in the dish."

Lester's lips pursed. *Yeah, not like your other son you named after Saint Francis, the patron saint of animals. Your son, Francis, the jackass.* Dutifully, he bit into a piece. The sweetness of his favorite chocolate could not erase the bitterness Lester held inside from his mother's choice of his brother over him. And yet, he was a dutiful son, never shrugging his obligation.

------

[15] Friend of "Bill" refers to Bill Watson who founded Alcoholics Anonymous. "White Ribbon" was a symbol of purity, temperance fleeing from alcohol.

CHAPTER 28

Gloria's contact at the Army Depot got her one pair of the patent leather boots Jean-Paul said was his best seller after the guns and munitions.

"This is going to make him do business with me," Gloria said. "What crazy fool would want patent leather boots in the desert?"

"That's really fucked up. I want to get this bastard behind bars so we can get to work on the other issue at hand," Lester said. The Desmond Vanderbilt murder weighing on him.

Gloria always said; "You never know what shadows lurk behind closed doors."

"What the hell is Jean-Paul going to do with one pair of boots? How are you going to handle an entire shipment once he says it's a go?"

"I'm working on the boot order. You don't know what I had to do to wrangle one pair. Not too many people ask for patent leather boots, just shoes. I have a meeting with him tomorrow. Want to come?" Gloria suggested to move away from Desmond Vanderbilt. She knew Ron Walker wasn't anywhere close to naming a person of interest. Forget about making an arrest.

Besides, Lester could walk and chew gum at the same time.

"I'd love to meet this bastard. He doesn't know me. I could be your inside contact. Let's do it."

"I was joking. I never told him about coming with someone else. So, it might work. We have a meet set up for 10 AM tomorrow morning. Pick me up at my place."

"See you then. I had a good time the other night."

"Me too, Lester, me too."

CHAPTER 29

Miami.

M orning came too fast for Lester, anticipating their meeting with the Miami Mercenary, Jean-Paul. Gloria was waiting outside her apartment building, right on time.

They knew their every move would be dissected, what they said and what they did. Although this was routine for them, coming from their military and police backgrounds, every movement, every word, had to be choreographed as if instructors at the Arthur Murray Ball Room Dance Studio taught it—smooth with no flaws.

That's why Gloria wore a sleek spaghetti strap, low cut white summer dress, as pristine as the Miami clouds and no bra. She knew what distracted men. Jean-Paul had continually looked at her breasts at the Wannamaker dinner party. She wanted Jean-Paul preoccupied so they could make a favorable deal.

Lester wore his tailored black pinstriped suit, along with his wide brimmed white Borsalino fedora. They had to play the part of their life in the underground world of darkness, including smuggling and murder. Their appearance fit right in with the Chicago mob of Al Capone, the Gentleman gangster.

Lester's sleek 1948 Series 62 Horizon Blue Caddy Convertible blended into the Miami sky, setting the stage as they rolled into the entrance of the most luxurious hotel in Miami, The Saxony, on famed Collins Avenue. The post cards in the lobby gift shop did not do justice to the ocean views. You couldn't smell the salt air or feel the warm sand between your toes from a shiny Kodachrome post card.

They were meeting in the hotel's lounge. Lester and Gloria's entrance made a statement that screamed money. Gloria held Lester back until they would be fifteen minutes late to the second.

Jean-Paul was already seated at the horseshoe shaped corner booth. Gloria made the introductions while Lester placed his hat on the bright red leather seat before shaking Jean-Paul's hand, giving the impression his hat was more important. Lester always sat facing the door. *Better to be safe than sorry, to be aware of who you may come face to face with.* Something he learned as a cop. It was a move mobsters used—looking over your shoulder all the time, not knowing if you'd been set up to be whacked.

Jean-Paul summoned the waiter to order drinks. "I know it's early , but you're passing through only one time. Life doesn't give you a dress rehearsal." Gloria slid in next to Jean-Paul, making it easier for him to get a closeup of what lie below the low-cut neckline of her dress. And her breasts did their job.

"I see you brought me a sample. Let's give a look," Jean-Paul was eager to transact business.

"They're perfect," he said, glancing down Gloria's low-cut neckline before holding up a boot and examining it. "Your supplier has quality." He glanced at Gloria in acknowledgement.

"Yes, they are perfect," Gloria said with a smug smile.

"It's what you're looking for, no?" Lester questioned.

"I could not ask for better," Jean-Paul said, tilting his head to the side with his eyes straying where Gloria intended. "These are better than the ones I've been getting." Enthralled with Gloria's posturing, Jean-Paul agreed to whatever she suggested, even to an increase of two dollars more per pair than he was currently paying.

"I will need 400 pairs to start. I'm not concerned about the price. How soon can I get them?"

Gloria needed to delay the order since she didn't have any patent leather boots or a source for more.

Is he putting us to the test, or does he really want 400 pairs out of the gate? Lester wondered.

Gloria moved closer to Jean-Paul. She was a master at maneuvering just so to stimulate his imagination. Turning, Gloria asked, "Lester, what do you think? Can you get this order filled for Jean-Paul?"

"Oh, oui, Monsieur, you are the supplier. I see. I thought you were Mademoiselle's *homme ami*. How you say, man friend?" He uttered a delighted chuckle, calculating his chances with Gloria for dishonorable intentions.

"That's me in person. I can handle your order. I consider your word good as gold, but we don't deal in gold, do we? So, I must insist on a deposit of, shall we say, five thousand dollars and the balance on delivery?"

"I can handle that. How do you get these boots and where?" Jean-Paul asked, not bothering to camouflage his desire to work directly with Lester's supplier.

"It does not matter, Jean-Paul. It's a simple supply and demand. You demand, I supply, you pay. Simple. Do we have a deal?" Lester asked, extending his hand to seal the deal as a gentleman's agreement. They could put nothing in writing. The transaction was for black market merchandise. Jean-Paul, without hesitation, extended his hand.

"Let's toast," Jean-Paul said, lifting his glass. "To a long business relationship and who knows what else." He grinned, revealing his mind was on making a separate deal with Gloria. "I have to pick up my wife and catch a flight. So, excuse me. I must bid you farewell for now. I will be back in a few days and I'll contact you."

As soon as Jean-Paul left, Lester and Gloria knew they had to act.

Gloria knew exactly where Jean-Paul lived from tailing him. She and Lester left within minutes of Jean-Paul.

Palm trees lined the street leading to his modest apartment building. They located Jean-Paul's name and apartment number in the lobby registry and took the small elevator. Barely room for four people, it rose sluggishly after the doors closed, stopping at the designated floor with a slight bounce. It was a quiet atmosphere. If it weren't for the lush hallway carpeting, their footsteps would have drawn attention. Residents would have slid open peep holes in their doors to see who was there.

Lester had experience picking door locks from his days as a cop, making snap decisions on the spot, using as his excuse a suspicious smell or noise coming from behind a closed door. He kept his lock pick pin set in a pocket-sized case. With expertise and a skilled hand, he quickly opened the door. Hurriedly, they scoped out the rooms before starting their search.

"Shit!" Lester heard Gloria's whispered exclamation.

"What is it?" he asked, moving toward her voice.

"Holy shit! We've got to move fast. There's luggage in the hallway, ready to go. When Jean-Paul said he was going to pick up his wife to catch a flight, I wasn't expecting him to return home to get his bags."

"Where the hell is his wife?" Lester asked.

"Good question. She was with him at the Wanamaker's dinner party. That's where I met them. I'll take the bedroom. You start in the living room," Gloria quickly decided.

Lester heard voices at the front door. Without hesitation, he joined Gloria in the bedroom, putting his fingers over her lips, using the *shh* sign, pointing to the door as it opened. They tensed, drawing their weapons.

Gloria would not hesitate to squeeze the double action trigger on her revolver. They both had past encounters, fatalities to their credit, and could have notched their gun belts many times over.

"Millie, take the bags to the elevator. I have to pee. I'll be right behind you."

"Okay."

Lester and Gloria stood like a pair of store mannequins, frozen, with controlled breath. They heard the toilet flush; a lock click; and receding footsteps. They exhaled, able to breathe again.

"Oh, my God! That was too fucking close. Go check the peephole," Lester directed Gloria.

"They got in the elevator. We still need to hurry. Mrs. Laurent may have forgotten something. I don't believe it. Millie Sparks was here."

"That was Millie Sparks?" Lester questioned, adding two and two. "Well, I'll be a son-of-a-bitch. Mrs. Laurent is part of the deal. She's working with Jean-Paul. She may also be an assassin."

"Hurry, Lester, let's do a quick sweep of the place and hightail it outta here."

CHAPTER 30

Clematis Street

The aroma of Louise's coffee escaped into the hallway of the fifth-floor office. She always made extra for girls in the offices down the hall. "Louise. I don't know how you do it? The smell of your coffee is compelling," as they popped in for free coffee.

"Y'all help yourself. Take a donut back with you," Louise offered hospitably in her southern drawl.

"Jeez, Louise," Lester called out. You ought to charge for coffee and donuts. Would you bring me a cup, please? No donuts. Bring your steno pad. We have to make some notes."

"Comin' right up, Lester. Before we begin, Roslyn Wanamaker has called at least a dozen times. Each time, she's more upset. I told her we have things under control and not to do anything irrational. I tell you, Lester, she's a firecracker ready to be lit."

Louise settled in the chair opposite his desk. "Okay, ready. Do you have some juicy stuff?"

"Christ. I'm gonna have to soothe her feathers," Lester said.

Louise thought, *Lester, you can soothe my feathers anytime you want.*

"You know, Louise, there really isn't any juicy info. We met with Jean-Paul. He wants me to supply him with 400 pair of patent leather boots."

"You got yourself in a tight one this time. How are you going to wiggle out of this?"

"Gloria has to figure something out. Forget it. No notes. Get her on the phone."

The phone rang, alerting Louise to return to her post.

"Lester Caine Investigations. How may I help you? Hold the line, Lieutenant."

Lester knew immediately what Lieutenant was calling.

"Ron, it's Lester. What do you have?" Lester wanted to get right down to the brass tacks.

"We dug through every one of those fucking files and turned up nada. We could find no one or anything with or without threats, constituting a danger to Judge Vanderbilt. My eyes are bleary. I thought I was going blind."

"Are you telling me..."

"Stop right there, Lester. I know what you're gonna say. So, yeah. I was there with my men and with however many Miami cops they could spare, and we dug deep. All the files that could have pointed to a potential threat to the Judge just fell apart. People were dead, moved away, or had concrete alibis. I don't even want to think about some cop doing the Judge because of sloppy police work. You know too well how hard it is being a cop and you know how things get overlooked or evidence compromised. I have to talk to Mrs. Vanderbilt again. She can have Libby or H-2, or both, present. Lester, this investigation is going south."

"Alright. I'll set that up for you."

"Make it happen fast."

"Any familiar faces from the photos you took at the cemetery?

"No, God damn it! I was hoping. I want Mrs. Vanderbilt to look at them. You should too, Lester. I'd appreciate that."

"I'll touch base with you, Ron."

Lester heard the all too familiar sound of a dial tone.

He buzzed Louise. "Get Scarecrow on the line."

Louise called "No answer."

"Keep trying." Lester snapped, tapping his desk rhythmically with a pencil, back and forth like an overloaded seesaw hitting the ground.

CHAPTER 31

Palm Beach-Police Headquarters.

Libby and H-2 accompanied Lorraine into the Palm Beach Island Police HQ as requested by Lieutenant Walker, who was ready for their arrival. Lester was waiting alongside Ron. Both men rose to greet them.

"Lester, I'm glad to see you. Thank you for coming. I haven't forgotten Pamela, you know." She smiled to share their secret. Everyone but Lorraine and Lester looked at each other quizzically, wondering what that meant.

"Thank you, Lorraine. I'll keep that in mind. Now, I'm here for you."

"Mrs. Vanderbilt, here are photographs we took at the cemetery. I want you to look at them to see if there's anyone you recognize. Take your time," Ron said, laying down each photo. Slowly, he arranged the photos in precise columns, row after row, like soldiers ready for morning inspection.

"Take your time, Lorraine," Libby repeated. "We're not in any hurry. Would you like water or coffee?"

"Coffee would be welcome," Lorraine answered in her soft, alluring voice. One by one, she picked up each photo from the line to get a better look, like the Drill Sergeant screaming in the soldier's face—so close he couldn't fit bad breath between them. She examined the face in each photo, sipping her coffee, dragging on her long Pall Mall cigarette stained with her red lipstick. She wanted no mistakes identifying or not the person staring back at her.

"No! No! No!" She pushed the photos back in place, one after the other, until the full array of photos returned to perfect formation. Then, hesitantly, Lorraine returned to a photo, pulling it back to her.

"Mrs. Vanderbilt, please take your time. Do you recognize this man?" Walker asked.

"Lieutenant, I know who has been to my home. This man has. He was with the catering business for our last fund raiser. Desmond had many friends, business associates, coworkers, and partners. I can identify everyone who has been to our home, and we had over one-hundred guests at our twice a year parties for The Children's Hospital, Desmond's favorite charity. Some people call it a photographic memory. I can remember faces at my shows back in the day. This man definitely was on the caterer's staff. His name was Tom or something like that and the caterer was Dilly Dally Deli Catering."

"We'll get right on that, Mrs. Vanderbilt. Are you up to looking at the photos one more time? Just to be absolutely sure," Walker said.

Lorraine released a plume of smoke from deep within her lungs. It mixed with the other cigarette smoke filling the small room, enclosing the five of them.

"I don't need to, Lieutenant. I just did. Are we through here?" she asked.

"If you're sure, Mrs. Vanderbilt, then yes, we are through. Thank you for coming in."

"Lester, do you mind taking me home?" Lorraine asked.

"Of course, Lorraine. It would be my pleasure."

"Lorraine, Libby and I are at your disposal if there is anything you need or want us to look into," H-2 said.

"Lorraine, we haven't finished looking through everything in Desmond's study as you asked me to do with you," Libby said.

"We'll get back to it, Libby. I'm not up to it right now and I know you're busy at the firm. I will call you."

1868 Wilshire Court

Lorraine Vanderbilt's Estate

Palm Beach Island is the *crème de la crème* of Florida and possibly of the entire United States, housing the nation's wealthy, including many industrialists who helped Florida's expansion. Lorraine nor Desmond ever flaunted their affluence. Their humble beginnings taught them humility. Both were generous with their time and money, lending themselves to charitable groups. Lorraine sat on the Board of Directors of a Palm

Beach bank and chaired a charity for children, as Desmond had for *The Children's Hospital.* They gave of themselves without prejudice, but Desmond's death was certainly not without enmity, as evidenced by his murder.

"Lester, make us a drink while I get into something more comfortable, will you?"

"I will. I'll be out by the pool."

"Oh, hello, Mr. Caine. I thought I heard voices. I got kinda spooked. You know, since Mr. Vanderbilt," the housekeeper mumbled, making the sign of the cross. Rosemary startled Lester, and he swung around, grabbing at his revolver.

"Hello, Rosemary. It's good to see you stayed on to help Mrs. Vanderbilt under the circumstances," Lester answered, closing his jacket to concealhis gun.

"Oh, I couldn't leave Miss Lorraine. I have been with them for many years. I wouldn't know where to go. They're my family." She dabbed at her eyes with a tissue she pulled from her sleeve.

"Rosemary, we'll be sitting pool side. Will you be so kind and make us a snack?" Lorraine asked. "And bring my checkbook."

"Of course, Miss Lorraine."

"Lester, I've been thinking."

"About?"

"Well, this might be nothing. I don't know if it's just me or am I picking up vibes from Libby? She's always at the ready to help me search through Desmond's things. She claims it's just 'to be sure.' She *suggested* Desmond could have stashed some important papers somewhere by accident and forgot about them. Desmond forgot nothing. He had a fantastic memory and believed in a place for everything. I've been around the block a few times, like you, Lester. I can pick up on things."

"I know you can recognize something if it doesn't smell right. You're one smart lady and savvy. You had to be to survive. If you think Libby's snooping, I can help you sort through Desmond's office," Lester said, appeasing Lorraine. *Libby wants to find that manilla envelope. That puts the icing on the cake. She and H-2 are in on whatever is in that envelope.*

"I'm not imagining this. Call it what you want; a woman's intuition, vibes, channeling, clairvoyance, or just plain street smarts. I feel it and can almost touch it, and I don't like it. Do you know what Libby's looking for?"

Lester didn't enjoy lying to Lorraine, but he did. "I can't imagine. Maybe it's a case they're working on that connects to the past. I wish I knew," Lester rambled, knowing damn well exactly what Libby wanted. He knew he had to get Scarecrow in on it, whatever it turned out to be. *I'll get that bastard. Desmond deserves no less.*

CHAPTER 32

Lester, guess who's on the phone?" Louise asked through the intercom.

"Louise, I really don't want to play any games. Just tell me."

You should only know the games I want to play with you. Images of Lester race through Louise's mind. *We could use blindfolds and handcuffs.*

"It's Scarecrow."

"Gloria, when are we going to meet and when are you going to pick up where we left off when you were going to tell me what was so important before my mother's panicky call?"

"Right now," ignoring his sarcasm and getting right to the point. "Are you sitting? I tailed Roslyn to the Burdines Men's Department. She had a gun ready to kill Millie Sparks. She needs to get slapped a few times."

"What! She had a gun? What the hell is wrong with her? I'll call her and tell her we will drop the case if she keeps this stupid shit up. Did you?" Lester asked.

"What, slap her? I should have. I took the gun and told her I would arrest her."

"What a stupid son-of-a-bitch. She is off the rails. She makes me fuckin' crazy! I have to cool down. How goes it with Jean-Paul and the boot order? We've got to rope this in before Roslyn gets herself killed by the Mercenaries for hire. This group has no conscience."

"Okay. We can meet Jean-Paul and go over things with him. I have a way to stall him. I'll set it up." Gloria said.

"Gloria, we need to get a move—"

"Lester, this bastard is not going anywhere," knowing exactly what Lester was after—the King Fish of them all—Desmond's murderer. "I want to help you with that one too. When the time is right, we'll hang the bastard by his balls."

"Gloria, we can't let this get fucked up. This is important for me and for you. We're well past the first forty-eight hours of a homicide—the most important first hours. Too much time slips away means the killer has more opportunity to slip away."

"I know, Lester. I promise you. I will call you as soon as I get word about the boots."

"Okay. I take you on your word. I'm going to call Roslyn and rip her a new—"

"I have a better idea," Gloria said. "Why don't you rip me a new one tonight and not waste your time on Roslyn? I'll bring Chinese and be at your place around eight."

"I'll have your martini chilled and ready," Lester said, feeling better already. *I better get another check from Roslyn before she winds up dead or in jail.*

CHAPTER 33

Miami.

Gloria and Lester arrived at the Saxony Hotel to meet Jean-Paul. He sat in the same booth as when they first met. Lester knew why Jean-Paul chose that booth. Once again, what he learned from the mobsters he'd collared and sent to prison rang true. Always sit facing the door. You never knew what or who would come through that door and maybe kill you.

Lester's suspicious eyes darted around the room. Usually there were bodyguards with the Boss that sat in the shadows. It's the same trick undercover cops use, and there they were. Two of his henchmen sat at a table directly behind Jean-Paul, an eagle's view where they could quickly get him to safety if need be.

"It's good that you could both make it," Jean-Paul said, rising. "I hope you have good news for me. My buyers are anxious. I want to move on to bigger business, perhaps with you both."

He's testing us, and we're not doing very well. Don't blow this, Lester thought.

"Yes and no," Gloria said. "We have the four hundred pairs of boots—"

"Patent leather boots, right?" Jean-Paul said, wanting reassurance.

"Yes. We have them, but they went to the wrong warehouse. They're stuck there until we can get proper releases. Military Red Tape. It shouldn't be too long," Lester said, waiting for the proverbial shoe-to-drop.

"How long?" Jean-Paul asked, his voice sharp and eyes narrowed. "You said you could deliver on time."

"Don't get your panties in a knot," Gloria said. "We said we'll deliver and we will. There was an unexpected hiccough. We have bigger things to talk about," she said, a master of misdirection.

"What is bigger than our deal?" Jean-Paul asked, compressing his lips.

"Your card says you are a Mercenary and gun for hire," Lester said.

"Yeah, so? For foreign countries. What are you asking?" Jean-Paul said.

"We have a need for that service," Gloria said. "Something local."

Jean-Paul looked at his two bodyguards, gave them a come-on head motion. He looked Lester in the eye. "Stand up. You know I have to check."

Lester knew he was checking for a wire in case he was undercover police. He complied. He breathed a little easier when they didn't check his ankle strapped with his.38

160

"Sorry, sister," the henchman said with a smirk, expecting Gloria to stand for a quick hands-on search.

"Don't keep your hands on the merchandise too long if you know what's good for you," Gloria said with a glare and stood.

"They're clean, Boss."

Lester thought, *if his cops had conducted a search like they did, hesitating to frisk Gloria because she was a woman, he would have had them transferred to parking meter detail. How could Jean-Paul have such stupid, non-thinking men around him?*

"I'm listening," Jean-Paul said.

"This person is in the way of us making tons of cash. This will be good for your business too. With this person gone, it opens the door for us, including you, to make more money than you can dream of."

"Okay, what is this great business deal you speak of?" Jean-Paul said, greed making his eyes gleam as he waited for more.

"We need someone removed. Simple as that," Gloria said.

"A request like that is not simple. It takes a lot of planning—who, what, where, and when. It takes finesse—getting the mark in the right situation without them knowing what is going to happen to them—and the talent to know how to do the job and dispose of the problem, leaving no traces of evidence. This is a professional business, the business of eliminating someone, so no one will ever find them, which, I assume, is what you want when you say you need someone removed."

"Yes. That's exactly it," Gloria said.

"Can we rely on you?" Lester asked.

"For a fee, and my fees vary, starting at fifty large. It could be more, never less."

"Here it is. We need an Army Colonel taken out. He's the one fucking up things for the delay," Gloria stated, staring into Jean-Paul's eyes. "With him out of the picture, we have someone willing to take his position and work with us. He'll oversee all the Army surplus we can get our hands on, including patent leather boots for the desert soldiers. Can handle this? We need to know before we proceed," taking a shot at what she hoped Jean-Paul would agree to. "This could lead to munitions and more."

Jean-Paul reached for Gloria's hand, and Lester grabbed it in mid-reach. Jean-Paul's goons stood and took a step forward before he waved them away.

"Some things don't cross the line," Lester said, not releasing his grip. He looked into Jean-Paul's eyes with a hard-ass stare, waiting for his nod of agreement before he released his powerful hold.

"I'll do this for the fifty-thousand because of what it will bring us all. Give me all the details and, of course, a down payment, as you asked me. Nothing in writing. When you have it all together, not in pieces, call me. We need to move on this. I need those boots."

Waiting for the valet to bring Lester's Caddy, he turned to Gloria; "You really dug deep on this one. He bought it. Now what?"

"It bought us time, didn't it?" Diverting Jean-Paul from the boots had been a trick she learned from her father, an amateur magician. He always said, 'Every magician has a girlfriend called Miss Direction.' Gloria had learned very early about her father's girlfriend.

CHAPTER 34

Palm Beach.

Lieutenant Walker walked into the Dilly Dally Deli Catering store on Worth Avenue, Palm Beach Island.

"I'm Lieutenant Walker," flashing what had defined him most of his life—his gold shield. "I need to speak with the owner."

"I'm the owner, Dilbert Dally. How can I help you?"

Ron grinned, not expecting Dilbert's greeting.

"I know," Mr. Dally said. "I cashed in on the name. It works. What brings you in, Lieutenant? Can I cater the Palm Beach Police annual picnic or Christmas party? I'll give you a good deal."

"I'll tell you what, Mr. Dally. When we have an annual picnic or Christmas party, I'll consider your offer." He handed him the photo Lorraine had pointed to

"Do you know this guy?"

Mr. Dally put his glasses on to get a better look and nodded; "Yes, yes. It's been a while, but he worked for me for a brief time. A real nice young man, polite, good with the customers, and he was a fast learner. He was always first to arrive and last to leave. That says a lot about a person, don't you agree?" Dilbert paused, but he didn't expect an answer. "He could have become a manager in no time, but he said he had to return to Miami. He got a better job offer. I won't hold no one back from bettering themselves, you know, Lieutenant. That was about a year ago, give or take, I might add. "

"Did he say where he was going? Do you have any info, you know, his address, telephone number, anything?" Walker asked.

"Let me look. C'mon on back, Lieutenant."

"Ah, here it is," Mr. Dally rummaged through a Rolodex, removed a card, and handed it to Walker.

"I need to write this down," he mumbled.

"No need, Lieutenant, you can have it. He's not coming back. He knew what he wanted, and it seems he'll get it. He had a tough childhood, in a way. After his father's accident, his mother married a man who became wealthy—something to do with a factory for the war effort. His stepfather adopted him, even though he was just shy of becoming a teenager. He grew up during a kid's important years without a father. His mother sent him away to the best schools, but that's cold. Kind of sad, don't you think? He's smart and has a lot going for him, but he was a loner, seemed distant, and lost. You get what I'm saying, don't you, Lieutenant?" Mr. Dally asked.

"I think I do. He ever talk about his father's accident? Mention any details?" Ron asked.

"No, short and to the point and to work. Oh, something else, Lieutenant. He was always reading those detective magazines on his break. He loved the forensic science. I asked him about it. He said his father's murder sparked an interest. You never know what's in people's heads, do you? Sad, very sad," Mr. Dally shook his head.

"Accident? Murder is no accident where I come from," Walker corrected Mr. Dally with disdain. "I'll need a list of all the catering jobs he was on. How long will that take?"

"Not long. Have a cup of java, Lieutenant, on the house. I'll get on that for you. I see your point, Lieutenant. Murder is not an accident."

Walker drank enough coffee on investigations and stakeouts throughout his career to keep him awake hours at a time. He rated the coffee and boasted he could tell where the coffee beans came from for each cup he drank. Dilly Dally's coffee was now at the top of Ron's list.

"Here you are Lieutenant. I hope this helps you," Dilbert Dally handed Ron the list of jobs he asked about.

"Thank you, Mr. Dally. You've been very helpful. I'll finish up here in a moment and see my way out."

"Take your time, Lieutenant. Can I get you more coffee?"

"Sure thing. Best coffee I've had to date, thank you. Oh, Mr. Dally, did he say where in Miami he was going to work by any chance?"

"Actually, Lieutenant, he did. He said he had a connection in some fancy restaurant...Silver or something like that. I don't go to Miami much, so I don't know about it. I'm too busy running my business."

"Mr. Dally, you've been a great help. Thank you and thank you for the coffee."

"You betcha. Anytime, Lieutenant, and remember about my discount."

Ron smiled, nodded, and waved his hand in a gesture of saying *sure thing*.

So, we have a suspect! Ron sipped his coffee and took out the pen his wife gave to him when he made detective, a 12K gold-filled ball-point. She told him she wanted it to match his gold badge. He clicked the barrel to lower the point and circled the phone number on the card. He stiffened when he read the address, then circled it two times with bold strokes.

"Vanderbilt residence," Rosemary answered the phone.

"Is Mrs. Vanderbilt there? It's the Lieutenant from the Palm Beach Police."

"Yes, Lieutenant, have you found the murderer?" Lorraine asked.

"No, Mrs. Vanderbilt. But I have a question. Do you know anyone by the name of Thomas Fairchild?"

"I know the Fairchild name, Lieutenant. That was a big case Desmond worked. Why? What does Fairchild have to do with Desmond's unsolved murder?"

Ron froze each time he heard "unsolved." *Every murder has to be solved on my watch.*

"What do you know about the name, Mrs. Vanderbilt?"

"It was a highly publicized case. One of Desmond's biggest. Maybe you don't know about it. It was in Miami, years ago, when he was just starting out. That's how Desmond and I met. He came to *Cleopatra,* the club I was working at. He and his partners were celebrating his victory. They got a priest, Father Timothy Fairchild, and his mistress acquitted of a murder charge. The jury agreed it was self-defense. The Archdiocese supported the priest and funded it all. It made all the papers, even the Italian papers. You know, because of the Vatican. That case made Desmond's firm a ton of money. After the ex-priest married his mistress, Desmond got him a position in the munitions factory he and his partners established for the war effort. They all got wealthy. Desmond even more so. "

"Jesus H Christ," Ron whispered.

"I'm sorry, Lieutenant, did you say something?" Lorraine asked.

"No. I'm just thinking out loud. A habit I have. Thank you, Mrs. Vanderbilt. I'll be in touch. If there is anything else you can remember that we haven't touched on, please call me."

"You'll be the first," Lorraine said, but thought, *no, I'll call Lester first, and right now.*

Lester was dialing Roslyn Wanamaker. Then he had to speak to Scarecrow. *I've got to get Gloria back on track for that goddamn crazy Roslyn and our Mercenary for hire. Roslyn has to stop popping in unexpectedly, waiting for me to get back here.*

"Lester, it's Lorraine Vanderbilt for you," Louise announced through the intercom.

"Lorraine, it's Lester."

"Lester, I just got off the phone with Lieutenant Walker," she said with a sob.

Lorraine was crying.

Jesus Christ, when it rains, it pours. "Lorraine, take a breath. Do you need me to come over?"

"Would you? I would appreciate that." She sniffled and drew uneven, shallow breaths.

Lester drove his Caddy into the circular driveway, not knowing what he was walking into. *Why hadn't Ron called him before Lorraine? What did he find?*

Rosemary answered the door before the bell chimes finished ringing its usual eight chimes. "She's out by the pool, Mr. Caine."

"Is she decent?" he asked.

"I told her you were here as soon as I heard the doorbell. She put her robe on. She's waiting for you. Would you like a drink, Mr. Caine?"

"I sure would, Rosemary. That would be great," Lester answered, looking to be sure Lorraine was wearing her robe before he stepped out to the patio.

"Lorraine?"

"I'm here, Lester. Sit, relax, take off your jacket, loosen your tie."

"Here you are, Mr. Caine," Rosemary said, handing Lester his drink, and turning back to the house.

"Rosemary, I'll take another." Lorraine held up her glass, polite and yet conveying she was Rosemary's employer.

"Right away, Miss Lorraine."

"Ah, that's good," Lester said. The bourbon rolled over his tongue with just enough ice to give it the exact chill for easy sipping. "Okay, Lorraine, tell me what Lieutenant Walker said that upset you and what he asked you."

Lorraine repeated the conversation between her and Walker. It took some thought to understand between Lorraine's tears. She convinced Lester this was a powerful lead to Desmond's murder.

He reassured her that this was one step closer to getting the son-of-a bitch, whoever Thomas Fairchild was. Lester finished his second Bourbon.

Lorraine swung her legs over the side of the chaise and stood. Her robe parted, and he glimpsed a light-colored thatch of hair at the apex of her long legs.

Lorraine had a great body, and Lester certainly enjoyed looking at her.

"Lester, Libby is still at it. Pestering me to let her come and continue to rummage through the house. She's making me uneasy."

"Tell her you're not ready and there's nothing you need now. Stick to your guns," he said before stepping into his Caddy. "My offer's still good. If you want, I'll go through everything with you." Libby's search would be fruitless. He had the envelope in his safe.

"Okay, Lester. I'll be strong."

"Good girl."

Lorraine pushed the heavy car door closed, leaned over, and gave Lester a kiss on his cheek. He inhaled a heady mixture of suntan lotion and Lorraine's perfume. "Thank you, Lester. You're a good friend."

CHAPTER 35

]]9

L ouise mustered all the info Lester had requested and created a folder. She placed it in the center of his desk, waiting for Lester's eyes.

"Ah! You got it. Thank you, Louise." *Here it is, in black and white. Creative name,* he thought. *The small munitions factory Desmond, his mentors, and his partners started up to support the US war effort had made many people wealthy.*

Miaflo Assembly Co.

Miaflo Assembly Co.

73 West Flagler Street

Miami, Florida

Principals:

- Desmond Vanderbilt

- Libby St. James

- Henry Harper

- Dasby Warner

- Harris Bleakly

Industry:

- Manufacturing and assembly

Start:

December 8, 1939

Louise had found a brief newspaper article on microfilm at the library. A photo showed all the principals cutting a ribbon for the opening of the new manufacturing and assembly factory. It would employ one hundred people, helping families during hard times and giving Miami a *shot in the arm*. Little did the reporter know that what was being manufactured and assembled would eventually give someone more than a *shot in the arm*.

Lorraine had told him that Libby, H-2, Desmond, Dasby, and Harris's connections could keep Miaflo's operations on the down-low. They disguised its real purpose—supplying the Naval Amphibious Training Base 128 miles north in Ft. Pierce, the Naval station training 40,000 troops to invade Normandy. The United States and Florida knew about the troops and training base. What they didn't know was what was being manufactured and for whom. To keep up with the demand for ammunition, Miaflo operated around the clock, three eight-hour shifts. The US government did not want the identities or location of secret munitions factories known for fear of sabotage and destruction. The government scrutinized employees. They had to sign a non-disclosure agreement, complying with the idiom used by the US Office of War Information: "Loose lips sink ships."

There was nothing about any employees—the priest, Timothy Fairchild, or Cynthia Beall, now Mrs. Fairchild, or their positions with the Miaflo munitions factory. Lester knew they, too, became wealthy through Desmond's generosity. Desmond, Libby, and H-2's success stemmed from Desmond's defense of the Fairchilds. The partners had agreed to give the ex-priest and his lady love a new start. Louise's research convinced Lester that Thomas Fairchild, son of Mrs. Cynthia Beall, was the primary murder suspect.

"Lieutenant Walker." He answered Lester's call in his usual manner.

"Ron, it's Lester. I just left Mrs. Vanderbilt. She gave me the whole rundown. It looks like we have our suspect. Our murderer, by all indications, is Thomas Fairchild. Revenge is his motive."

"And the catering owner told me he read detective stories and studied crime scenes in those tell-all detective magazines,"

"That explains why the crime scene was so clean except for the foot print your men found. He read up on how to go about committing what he thinks is a perfect murder," Lester said.

"He apparently has no consideration for his mother. I bet he doesn't even see her or his stepfather, the former priest," Ron said. "He takes what he sees as blood money, probably thinks they dole it out to ease their conscience. In his mind, they murdered his father in cold blood."

"Now, we have to find him. I've already put out an APB[16]. I've got a good lead, thanks to Mrs. Vanderbilt's selection of that one photo and you suggesting I contact the catering company the Vanderbilts used. Mr. Fairchild was an employee and may work in a Miami restaurant with *Silver* in its name. We've got a team in Miami looking for him as we speak."

"Ron, I'm with you one hundred percent. I'm going to need your help on another case I'm working. Conspiracy to commit murder. We'll talk soon."

"Don't change the subject. I want you to stay clear of any restaurant in Miami where this Thomas Fairchild is working and tell me before you do anything. Is that clear?" Ron was adamant. "Now tell me about this conspiracy murder case you're working."

Lester gave Ron the highlights of his plan, leaving out some minute details. He said just enough to get his help with a sting operation, but not to let Ron know who, what, or where.

"Jesus H Christ, Lester. All the crazies come knocking on your door. Retirement is supposed to be easy street."

---

[16] APB-All Points Bulletin for all police throughout the US.

"That's what *they* say, whoever *they* are. But *they* really don't know shit from Shinola, do they? I know the routine."

"Don't worry, I've got you covered."

Lester hung up before Walker could make any more demands, knowing full well it wasn't gonna happen. He knew from previous cases, Ron's sources were pretty divided. After the fact, he would be thankful for anything Lester would bring to him.

Where should I hunt this killer? What about our Mercenary? Where are we going to get the boots? Gloria, Gloria, Gloria!

CHAPTER 36

Gloria, we must get Jean-Paul under wraps and get the son-of-a-bitch in jail."

"Easier said than done, Lester. We set the stage for our plan"

"Yeah. I got Walker in on it. He's willing to be the patsy and pose as the Army Colonel that stands in our way."

"We have to nab him before Roslyn winds up with a bullet in her head."

"From the look and sounds of things, Gloria, Laurent's got a few notches on his handgun. Let's meet and put our heads together."

"Sounds like a plan," *but I want more than our heads together,* as business thoughts turned to lust. "My place or yours?" Gloria asked.

"Mine."

"The Hacienda Arms it is. I'll be there around eight. Get Chinese."

Before he could answer, Lester heard the dial tone. *What is it with her and fucking Chinese takeout?*

Gloria was fashionably late, as usual. Her military training had taught her to be on time, but she wasn't in the military any longer. She would show up as late as she wanted, but never enough to upset the host, unlike other women who took an hour when they said they'd be ready in five minutes. *What's the point of that?* She wondered. *If you're going to be an hour, say an hour.*

Gloria had fashionably late down to a science. She regarded an entrance as a statement, a ruse to make people recognize she had arrived. Timing was important. Lester knew this about her and timed the Chinese food to the exact ring of the doorbell.

"I don't know why you gave up a career in the limelight of stage and film. Look at you." Lester's eyes moved from the top of her head to her toes.

She stood five feet-six inches in a vee-neck black-and-white print spaghetti strap summer mini dress, showing just enough cleavage and spotlighting her long legs. She held her heels by their strap in one hand and a small purse in the other.

"You are beautiful"

"Thank you, Lester. My feet are killing me," giving him a peck on the lips.

"Sweet lips," Lester murmured. "I'll get the wine glasses. Food is ready. Walker said we should set this up, get Jean-Paul in position to pull the trigger."

"Sounds dangerous, Lester. Doesn't Jean-Paul have to tail him and know what Walker looks like? You know, get to know his M.O. so he has a plan to kill him?"

"That's impossible. How can Ron put himself out there? He can't walk away from his duties. We've got to set it up so we can be there with him. We have to convince Laurent there is no other way."

"I'm sorry, Lester," Gloria said with harshness. "He's a professional, and he will not change his way of doing things precisely down to seconds for the kill."

"We must make him believe it will be the only time. We'll tell him military personnel always surround the Colonel. He'll have to devise a way to get him alone. Timing will be all important."

"Tell Ron how dangerous this guy is. I know he's not a pussy, but he needs the facts. Let him back out if he wants. We can't make him a sitting duck!"

Gloria refilled her wineglass. Some of her best ideas came after a glass or two.

"Hmm. This might work, Lester. Let's hire another mercenary to act as the Colonel. Maybe we'll kill two birds with one stone."

"Maybe you need another refill, Gloria. You're not there yet," Lester said, knowing how she brainstormed. *But maybe I should give her idea some thought. Talk it over with Ron.*

"You know my favorite wine, cabernet Sauvignon, and my favorite drink, vodka martini. We may have a future together." She placed her glass down, leaning in to kiss him. "This doesn't mean I agree with you using Walker as our decoy. I don't have a good feeling about this."

"Maybe you'll have a better feeling about... this!"

CHAPTER 37

The phone rang like morning reveille awakening the troops.

"Jesus, Lester. Could you make that ring any louder? There's a dial on the bottom of the phone just for that. Jesus!"

Gloria adjusted her head already on Lester's chest, her arm across his stomach. She loved listening to his heartbeat, but this morning it raced from the jolt it got. The ring of the black rotary dial telephone was like the monster that hid in the closet waiting to jump out at you.

"Caine," Lester answered groggily. "Mom, this better be good."

"It's not *Mom, sweetheart*," a falsetto voice replied. "It's Ron. Must be nice to be retired and work for yourself," he gibed from the other end of the line. "I know you must have a lady friend or..."

"Don't even go there. What time is it?"

"Who cares?" Gloria whispered, reaching for the pack of Lucky Strike cigarettes on the night table.

"You got company, so I'll make it quick," Ron said. "This is a million to one shot."

Gloria eavesdropped on the conversation, her ear on Lester's chest. She continued moving her hand down his stomach, arousing him.

"Oops, look what I found," she said, taking a drag and looking for the ashtray.

Lester shifted under the sheets, grabbing Gloria's hair as she kissed his stomach and moved her head lower, exhaling a smoke ring and mimicking contestants at a carnival tossing rings onto a pole.

Lester pulled her up as Ron continued to babble. "I'm still here, Ron, waiting for the reason for my wake-up call."

"We've got a lead on Thomas Fairchild. We've set up surveillance in Miami.

Lester sat up, throwing Gloria off. She rolled onto the floor with a thud.

"Are you all right, Lester? I heard a noise," Ron chuckled.

Gloria climbed back into bed, pulled back the sheets, and resumed where she left off.

"I'm still waiting, " Lester said, shaking his head at Gloria, trying to concentrate on Ron's telephone call. "So, are you gonna tell me what you have?"

Gloria stopped teasing when Lester's seriousness finally registered. She reached for her smoke in the ashtray. "What?" she whispered, shifting closer so she could hear.

"Who do you have in custody? You've got to repeat that," Lester said.

"We found him—Thomas Fairchild, thanks to you and Mrs. Vanderbilt pointing him out in the photo line-up. We found him in Miami. He's working at the Silver Slipper as the sommelier.[17] He's not in custody yet."

Lester knew the *Silver Slipper* well. It was notorious for mobsters from around the country. They met there and used it as a national message center. The entertainment was top-notch and attracted movie stars, singers, politicians, and anyone who wanted to rub elbows with the who's who and had the bucks to dine. The restaurant was famous for its Blue Crab Meatballs and spaghetti.

"I'm...I'm speechless," Lester swung his legs over the side of the bed.

"Let me tell you, Lester. It's a good thing we got to him before *they* did." Lester knew who Ron meant. "Mr. Fairchild would be filleted, chopped, and fed to the fishes if they got a whiff that he murdered Desmond Vanderbilt."

Desmond had been their *Consigliere,* as they referred to him. Their advisor and attorney, along with Libby and H-2.

"I'm shell shocked, Ron."

---

[17] Sommelier is a wine steward trained and knowledgeable professionally in all aspects of wine.

"Here's the rub."

"There's more?" Lester questioned. Gloria grabbed hold of the receiver to hear the last shoe drop. She stubbed the tip of her cigarette in the ashtray, but not fully extinguished.

By now, Gloria had her hand wrapped around Lester's, each tugging the receiver closer to an ear.

"C'mon, Ron, you're killing us...me."

"I'm getting a search warrant for his apartment. Sorry, Caine. I can't let you in on this one. The captain is breathing down my neck."

"Understood." *That's more reason I should be there—my experience.* "You know where to find me."

Lieutenant Walker heard the dial tone, smiled, and hung up.

"Okay, Scarecrow, I bet you can't scare me!"

"We'll see about that..."

CHAPTER 38

St. Mary's Hospital,

West Palm Beach.

Lester's Caddy screeched to a halt in the parking lot, ignoring the No-Parking Zone signs and running into the Emergency Room.

"Where is she?" Lester demanded.

A uniformed officer who knew Lester signaled with his thumb at the cubicle with the closed curtain.

Lester pulled the curtain back and entered, oblivious to who was there or her state of dress.

"You'll have to wait outside," the attending physician said, looking up and compressing his lips.

"I'm not going anywhere," flashing his PI credentials and badge. "Louise, what the hell happened?"

"Look, I'll let you stay if you stand there quietly and let me do my job. Do you understand?" the doctor said.

"Lester, please. Listen to the Doctor. I'm alright. Just a scratch," Louise said.

"A bit more than a scratch. Five stitches should do it," he said, tying off the synthetic thread suture." I put them as close together as possible to keep scarring to a minimum."

"I know how to eliminate them, Doc. Thank you," Louise called to his retreating back.

"I got to the office earlier than usual," she said. "The door was ajar, and I heard noises. I called out, thinking it was you. The noise stopped. I opened my purse to reach for Edith and introduce her and wham! The next thing I know, Harry's propping me up on his mail bag and now I'm here. Someone was in the office."

Lester smiled. Edith was Louise's .38 snub nose revolver. She kept her close and was not afraid to have someone eat it. The code name Edith was born from Louise's earlier life. Lester wondered just how many notches Louise might have on Edith's handle.

"You're good to go," the doctor said, handing her a prescription. "You might have a headache. Fill this and follow the directions in case aspirin doesn't cut it."

"Thank you, Doctor."

"He's cute," Louise said as the nurse handed her release forms to sign.

"Yeah, he's married. Every nurse here has tried. Believe me."

"Who's Lester Caine?" An aide asked, pulling back the curtain.

"That's me."

"Telephone at the desk for you."

"Caine."

"Lester, it's Ron. I knew you'd be there. How's your gal doing?"

"Louise is doing great. She claims it's a scrape, but she has five stitches. She's a tough broad."

"Your mailman found her and called us. I have some uniforms doing the rounds and a fingerprint man. Maybe we can turn something up."

"Thanks Ron."

"We tried to serve the search warrant on Thomas Fairchild. He's in the wind. I don't know how he got word we had surveillance on him. I wanted you to know in case you come up with anything."

"I'll keep you in the loop. I have a hunch when we find who did this to Louise, it's going to be Thomas Fairchild."

Louise tugged on Lester's arm. "Let's go. Take me back to the office."

"No! I'm taking you home and putting you to bed."

"Promise?" Louise said, smiling like the cat that ate the canary.

Clematis Street.

Lester returned to his office after he settled Louise and they had a drink together. He wanted to be sure she was calm enough to stay alone. When Louise told him she'd see him in the office the next morning, he knew she would be okay.

He caught up with the uniforms as they finished going from office to office. No one had seen or heard anything at that early hour. He'd bet there wouldn't be any strange prints. Louise got blindsided. Maybe it was a good thing she spooked him, but she'd caught the brunt of it. If he hadn't got the jump on her, he'd have been a dead man.

Opening the door, it surprised Lester how neat everything was. No overturned furniture, files or desk drawers thrown around. Only one file drawer was open. He thumbed through the folders, drawer by drawer. Nothing seemed to be missing. He turned to check the Miaflo file he'd left on his desk. Still there, but it was open and turned sideways, as if someone had read it. He rushed to the cabinet that housed the safe—locked.

"Thank God," he blurted. This guy is good. He didn't take anything in case he got caught. There's no incriminating evidence.

By now, Lester was hungry, worn, and craved some solitude from all the pressing issues on his plate, including getting two killers off the street. And he needed to call his mother. Another contentious call. She'd remind him 'truth hurts.' Mired in the Jean-Paul mess and Desmond's murder, he was spinning his wheels.

Lester took his surly self to Lola's for healing vibes, his favorite watering hole on Royal Palm Way. Lola's was a jazz club featuring Midnight Train. The soulful smooth jazz ensemble played the mellow sounds that oozed cool and featured the expressive voice of the lovely vamp, Claudette Moreau, a French Creole.

Claudette's pitch, timbre, and controlled vibrato invited your heart into hers. She said without words, "Become one with me." On drums, Dino Dees; piano, Harry 'Fingers' Johnson; saxophone, Charlie Barber; trumpet, Bobby 'Lips' Malloy; bass, Clarence Boyer; guitar, Pete Stringer. Together they melted your troubles away like Lester's only drink—the delicate DNA of Jim Beam Bourbon.

This was miles from the cop bars Lester would rarely go to. Too many cops unwinding in a bottle with war stories were not for him.

Lola's was Lester's favorite place to unwind and imbibe. He liked the ambience, the music and, of course, there was Claudette, Lester's favorite squeeze, away from Gloria.

Regulars crowded the bar, joined by newbies who heard the buzz and wanted to see what it was all about. It didn't matter what night of the week. The two barkeeps kept the bar pristine. Ramona and Carl dressed in evening wear—white shirts, black bow ties, vests and tuxedo pants, complete with a satin stripe down the outer seam. Lester entered with a confident stride he'd be welcome.

Carl looked over at Ramona and said, "Here comes trouble, and Miss Calliope's with him."

"Tall, dark and handsome. Kind of trouble I wouldn't mind waking up next to," Ramona whispered. "Lester, you look like the horse that came in here last night. Why the long face?" Ramona asked, pouring his Jim Beam.

"Ramona, you always make me smile."

"Some guy was in here last night asking about you. He peeled off a C-Note from the stack his clip held and slid it to me. I shrugged him off. You come in now and then I told him and pushed the hundred back toward him. He knew you came here, so I couldn't deny it, you handsome devil, you. Claudette is one lucky lady. If things don't work out with you two...," Ramona touched his hand. "He left in a huff. Left me the hundred."

"Is this him?" Lester pulled Thomas Fairchild's photo from the inner pocket of his suit jacket and laid it on the bar."

Ramona glanced at the photo, continuing to mix drink orders.

"That's him. Looks a little older in person."

"If he comes in again, call me. Don't deal with him. He's not nice. I don't know what he'll do."

"If you're carrying his photo, should I be worried? I carry a Beretta .25," tapping her right pocket.

"Keep that to yourself, Ramona. That can do some real damage. No one needs to know. Yes, keep it with you. Not for him–just, you know, peace of mind."

Applause interrupted the chatter in the room.

"She's up, Lester. She's scouring the audience for you."

Servers hurried to keep pace with orders. The temperature rose with standing room only, compressing the room. Once Claudette saw Lester at the bar, she would start the show with Where or When, a song with romantic lyrics suggesting a relationship going nowhere, although meeting over and over. That suited Claudette just fine. The night was young and closing was a long way off before Lester and Claudette would set fire to the sheets.

Savoring the bourbon rolling over his tongue, the thought of what Louise said when he was going to take her home from the hospital hit him as if he'd seen a ghost. Might have been the medication.... Claudette blew him a soft kiss, and he succumbed to her soulful reach, dismissing Louise.

They always invited Lester to the stage, bringing Calliope[18] with him—his prize 1940 French Besson Brevete trumpet. Lester knew how to blow a mean jazz piece, often using a Harmon copper mute, breathing a breath into the bell to hold it in tight like making love to a beautiful woman. Only here, as in the past, Lester's love making was with Miss Calliope. He would play 'til the wee hours of the morning just like in the New York jazz clubs. The healing just began for Lester.

---

[18] Calliope was the most prominent of the Greek goddesses who presided over poetry and song.

CHAPTER 39

L ouise came to the office the next morning like the trooper she was. Life's vicissitudes had played havoc with her, but molded her into a strong, determined, and loyal woman, unlike her mother who had ridden off into the sunset with a stranger and abandoned her family.

She was grateful to Lester for hiring her on the spot. He provided some perks besides a handsome salary like paying her home telephone and occasional medical bills, and a savings account he started for her. He set it up so she couldn't get to it until her later years. Louise still had maternal instincts for her two younger sisters, sometimes giving them a needed helping hand. Both had married drinkers who worked sporadically, replicating the psychological effects their father had on them. Louise had seen through it all. She saw Lester as one of the last good guys. Her hope for a chance to love him without commitment never dimmed. The thought continually crossed her mind.

Lester wasn't through the door before Louise greeted him.

"We're in good shape. The office wasn't ransacked. What the hell was he after?"

"Are you sure you're okay to be back?" When she turned her head, he saw the stark white bandage covering her stitches. She'd artfully combed her hair to conceal most of it."

"I'm sure. No more talk about it."

"Call the locksmith and get the locks changed. It appears he was looking for files. He took nothing. My hunch is he wanted to know what we found at the judge's murder scene. I think he was in the crowd outside the Vanderbilt's house the day I arrived. That's how he found out who I was and why I was there. Once he knew, he put a tail on me. He was at *Lola's* the other night asking about me. He's shrewd. Sources say he's studied up on crime scenes."

"That little bastard! I wish I could have introduced him to Edith."

Lester raised his eyebrows, wrinkling his brow at the thought. *She meant it. She really might have a few notches on the handle of her.38 from her past. I can't imagine how many bodies are buried out in the Everglades. Knowing her dark childhood, maybe one or two of hers.*

"Louise, get Libby for me, will you?"

"On the line, Lester."

"Libby—"

"Lester, how are you? Lorraine tells me you've been wonderful, helping her work through her grief. Is there something you need?"

"Actually, yes. Lorraine told me you keep after her to go through Desmond's things with you. Why?"

He heard her sigh. "I wanted to be sure she missed nothing we needed. We've known Desmond squirreled things away. You know, for later use in a case he may have been working on."

Lester knew that was bullshit. "Libby, you know as well as I if there is any information, it would be in the case file or in the hands of opposing attorneys for discovery. He hasn't practiced for a while, Libby, and the pressure on Lorraine makes her uncomfortable. She's asked me to help her." *Might as well find out if one and one still equals two,* wanting to hear her reaction.

"Oh...I can't imagine why. She doesn't know what we may need in our office, and neither do you."

That clenched it for Lester. She just confirmed she was looking for that envelope.

"No need to upset her now. She's pretty fragile, so I think we should let sleeping dogs lie."

"For now," Libby snarled, hanging up.

Before he could replace the receiver, Louise was on the intercom.

"Lieutenant Walker, on the line."

"Lester, can you come over? I got photos off the wire from the FBI's surveillance of the Silver Slipper. They're monitoring the activity of some of Miami's least respected citizens. You know, the mobsters' coming and goings. That place is like a revolving door. They're asking for our help identifying the faces in the photos. I'd like you to look. I'm staring at one that we've identified."

Palm Beach Police headquarters.

Bert, the desk Sergeant greeted Lester with his usual dyspeptic expression.

Maybe I should buy him a bottle of Tums. You'd think days away from retirement, he would look forward to fishing, or being on his boat. Lester reflected. *Maybe not. I could have retired and lived the life of Riley, but chose not to.*

"Go ahead, Caine. He's waiting for you," Bert signaled with his thumb like he was hitchhiking.

"In here," shouted Walker. "Take a look at these. Got 'em on the table already."

"Well, I'll be a son-of-a-bitch," Lester exclaimed. "You know this one," pointing to the photo of the man Lorraine identified as Thomas Fairchild.

"And this one," Lester pointed, "is Jean-Paul Laurent, the Mercenary who's going to assassinate our inside Army colonel—you—in our sting. The woman next to him is the client who claims her husband, a prominent vascular surgeon, is plotting to have her killed. That's the one I told you I needed your help with. The Doc supposedly hired the man she's with to do the deed!"

"Jesus H Christ, Caine. How do all these fucking crazy people fall into your lap? When is all this supposed to take place? As if the captain's shit storm isn't enough, now the politicians are at it. They want action, calling and coming to the station. They want the Judge's killer."

"So do I, and so do you. Stop the shit, Ron. You know as well as I do that this Thomas Fairchild is the killer. We just need to find him."

"No shit, Sherlock. His apartment was clean. Nothing—empty. I told you, he's in the wind."

"He had to be the one who assaulted Louise and rummaged through my office, so he's still around. I can understand why Thomas Fairchild's photo is here. He worked at the Silver Slipper. But why is Laurent there? Why is my client there with him? What is she doing walking out to his car at the Silver Slipper?" Lester questioned.

"Now's the time to tell me all about your crazy client and this sting."

"Maybe we can get two birds with one stone. I have no fucking clue why my client, Roslyn Wanamaker, is with this Mercenary for hire, Jean-Paul Laurent, at the Silver Slipper where our suspect, Thomas Fairchild, was working. Jesus, what a triangle! Have your men questioned the staff?"

"The FBI intercepted us. They said they'll find out what they can and get back to us. They didn't want any suits around to interfere with their surveillance. You know their targets can spot suits a mile away. Besides, many of the staff have arrest records. We know them and vice versa. They know the detectives. So, we were canceled by the Iron Hand of the Bureau."

"Goddamn it!" Lester pounded his hand on the table.

"My sentiments exactly," Ron quipped. "Now how can I...we get two, maybe three birds with one stone? Caine, how the hell do you sleep at night?"

Lester thought about that. *A lot better when there's someone next to me.*

Claudette's words the morning after immediately came to mind. 'Lester, only two times last night. You must have a lot of cop shit on your mind. Maybe you should ease up on your cases. All work and no play... you know what happens? ... Lester is a dull boy.'

CHAPTER 40

Gloria's phone continued to ring, annoying her. Climbing out of the shower, she dash across the living room floor, dripping soap and water, grabbing at the towel, and trying not to slip. *Why, when you need to get there in a hurry, is walking a few feet like trying to reach the goalposts on the other end of the football field?*

"Hello," she snarled.

"It's me. We have a lot of work to do. The fat's in the fire. How long before you can meet me?"

"Hialeah. Give me an hour,"

Would he ever get used to conversations with no goodbyes? Whatever happened to civility? Lester listened to the dial tone.

Hialeah Race track.

This time, Lester had seats and was waiting. He knew Gloria would be fifteen minutes late, her M.O., so he bought the racing forms and coffee.

She showed up on schedule. She could have posed for *Vogue*, except a pouty frown replaced a smile. Lester considered an enigma he'd tried solving before—*Gloria, Claudette, Ramona, Lorraine, Louise. Louise? When did she make the list? Each one brings something to the table, but I don't want to take the plunge a third time. And Louise is too young. I shouldn't consider Louise. Maybe...definitely consider Ramona and Lorraine. ... Toss that out, Lester. Toss the whole damn thing out. Friends can be long lasting, but how long will the benefits last?* "Gloria, I have your espresso."

"It's twelve noon. You can toss it. Go get me a vodka and some of their caviar sweet toasted bread triangles," she ordered.

"You seem a little wound up."

"I thought we were going to have drinks the other night, and I never heard from you."

"So now I've got to pay with caviar? Something came up," thinking of his night with Claudette.

"There's the telephone. I know you have one. You've used it. Really, you have more than one. Don't let it happen again. Are we clear?"

"As mud. Let me get your order. I'll make it a double," he murmured.

"I heard that and you can go fuck yourself while you're at it."

Anatomically impossible, he smirked. *She'll go off like a cannon if I say that. I hope the vodka cuts the tension.* He ordered them both a double. *What's with Gloria's bitchiness? They both know their relationship is casual.*

"Here you go, honey. Don't choke on it," Lester said, handing her the toast and her drink."

"Cute, Lester. Real cute. Now that *you're* calm, you can take the honey bullshit and shove it. Don't placate me. He's tailing me. Don't look yet. Take the binoculars, look toward the tote board, then swing to the right. Guess who?"

"Yeah, he's tailing me too. Clever guy. He's gathering who, what, and where to see what we...or the police have on him. He's coming closer." He mustn't let it slip that Fairchild was at *Lola's* asking about him. *Lola's* was his private place, just for him, for the moment, and for Claudette.

"What do you mean, he's tailing you? You've said nothing. When?" Gloria demanded. "Lester, are we in this together or not?"

He squirmed with the double inference she may have made.

"He was following me in the car. I ditched him. And I just told you. Walker called me in. The FBI sent photos for him to see if we knew any of the mugs. One of them was ...get this...Jean-Paul Laurent, and...You're never gonna believe it...there's one of Roslyn Wanamaker."

"Wait! What? You're telling me the FBI has surveillance on all of them? Why?"

"They happened to be in the photos the Feds took at the Silver Slipper. They have surveillance on the club because of who comes and goes, civilians and mob guys. Our subjects got caught in the crosshairs. What are the chances? A million to one? This could not have dropped into our lap any better if we planned it." Lester gave Gloria the run down.

"Look at him. Nonchalant like he's some kind of professional. C'mon, Lester, let's approach this son-of-a-bitch. What do you say? I know you've got a set on you," Gloria expressed her continued beef against Lester.

"Not yet. I want to know his next move. He either thinks we're stupid or aren't on the top of our game." *He should only know.*

"Listen, Roslyn's giving me the runaround, trying to give me the slip. I'm hot on her tail again. She won't get far except us being together like we are now and were supposed to be the other night. So far, I have not seen her with Jean-Paul. That's hard to believe. What the fuck is she doing with him? This is getting too deep, deeper than I thought. For you too."

Gloria's tension hung in the air between them, thick enough to cut it with a knife.

"What the hell is going on with Walker and the Jean-Paul set up?" Gloria demanded.

"I'm working on it. Don't get your panties in a bunch."

"If you ever want to see these panties again, you better get your head on straight. What the hell does that mean...I'm working on it? Is Walker in or out? We need to cut through the bullshit here." She snapped at him like a yapping little dog. A couple nearby heard her raised voice and turned to look at them.

What the Hell is with her? I've never seen her in a tizzy like this.

"Did you see him turn, look this way?" Gloria asked.

"He wants us to spot him. Why else would he be so open? He's not stupid. He has something up his sleeve. That's why he broke into my office."

"Maybe he plans to kill us, or maybe you. He may have hoped to find you in your office instead of Louise. No, it must be both of us since he's seen us together. He knows who I am and we're about to put the squeeze on him. If he's all you say he is with a thirst for how detectives solve crimes, he should have joined the force. But why was Roslyn Wanamaker with the Mercenary for hire? And we must not forget Millie Sparks, who was with Jean-Paul's wife."

"Lester, this is getting crazier by the minute—our guy here, Roslyn, Jean-Paul and Millie. I've never seen anything like this and I bet you haven't either," Gloria rambled.

"I'll be right back. I'm going to get us another round. I'll even get you more caviar that I hate," Lester said. "Here, take these," handing Gloria the binoculars.

"Shit, he's gone," she shrilled.

"Give me those. Son-of-a-bitch. He's not there."

"So, now you're doubting me?" Gloria snapped.

"Let's go. You look in the lobby. I'll check the men's room. Be careful. He's dangerous."

"I've got my piece."

Within minutes, they met at the betting windows. To their surprise, Thomas Fairchild pulled a vanishing act. He had melted into the crowd.

"Lester, this is not good not seeing him. Let's get out of here."

"I'll walk you to your car. You can drive me to mine. I can't wait to nail the little bastard."

"This is your fault. You let him slip away," Gloria snarled.

CHAPTER 41

Palm Beach Police Headquarters

Lieutenant Walker finally got the go ahead from his captain to get on board Lester and Gloria's sting operation to nab Jean-Paul Laurent, Roslyn and Wayne Wanamaker, and Millie Sparks. They labeled it "Operation Desert Boots".

They set their meeting on the second floor, closed off to everyone having access to the building. Attending were Ron Walker, Lester, Gloria, and the captain. Lester reviewed the purpose of the sting and it had nothing to do with getting patent leather boots to the desert soldiers. It was about conspiracy to commit murder by Jean-Paul Laurent of the fake Army Colonel, Lieutenant Ron Walker. Walker had stepped in to get the boots out of the Army inventory. Would their plan work?

"We've got to get this show on the road. Jean-Paul is anxious for these crazy patent leather boots for the desert army," Lester began.

"I've never heard of such ah...ah, I don't know what to call it," the captain said. "I've served in the Army and was overseas and I never heard of or saw soldiers with patent leather anything. Are you sure about this? Maybe he's testing you both to see how you can really pull something off."

"No, captain. This is for real. I got him a sample," Scarecrow said.

"Jesus Christ. What's the world coming to?" Shaking his head from side to side.

"What do we have so far?" Ron asked.

"You...we will meet at a high stakes' poker game with a thousand dollar buy in at an after-hours club in Miami. It's near the Cleopatra and owned by the same mobsters. They have armed security. We will stake you—don't worry. This is just for him to get to know you and how you play poker, and we hope you can. That tells volumes about a person and Jean-Paul knows how to read someone. So, not only do you have to play the cards you're dealt, you've got to play your cards into the sting. We have an inkling that Doctor Wanamaker may be there. Gloria and I will be by your side and help break the ice."

"I've got a pulse on our other suspect, Thomas Fairchild. He's holed up at the Princess Ann Hotel in Boca Raton," Gloria said.

"I'll call the Judge for an arrest warrant and get a team together to serve the paper," the captain said.

"Boca Raton? That's fitting," Walker said."

"Why?" Lester asked.

"Boca Raton, a Spanish term for rat's mouth," Gloria added.

CHAPTER 42

Clematis Street

The phones were ringing off the hook at Lester Caine Investigations. Louise answered one line while the second line lit up. When she answered line two, line one would ring. This went on for the first hour after Louise opened the office for the day. She hadn't even had time to put up a pot of coffee.

Each call was a repeat of the first from a reporter who had a good relationship with Lester, hoping for the scoop about what he had heard on the police scanners. Lester knew how to get his back scratched and scratch those in return. A simple rule of life–quid pro quo–this, for that, he learned well as a New York City beat cop working with his snitches and hookers. Lester would never not return the favor. He knew all too well the importance that information off the street played getting perps behind bars.

"Lester, thank God you're here. The phones are driving me crazy. Nonstop since they heard about the deaths over the wire. Do you know anything about it?"

"No."

"Miami police are on the scene of a triple homicide."

"What's that got to do with us?"

"Here's the address." Louise handed him the message. She waited for his reaction.

Lester stared at the piece of paper.

10328 W. Royal Palm Way

Miami, Florida

Lester knew the address well from Scarecrow. The address was that of Roslyn and Wayne Wanamaker in the gated community known as Palm Oaks. *Why the hell a developer would name the community Palm Oaks is beyond me. There is no such tree.*

"Oh, my God! No, it can't be. Is this right?"

"That's the info the first reporter gave me and confirmed by the others. Hard to believe, isn't it? Want me to go with you?" Louise hoped to see the details first hand.

"I need you here to handle these phones, and who knows who will knock on the door? Keep Edith close at hand. Get me Walker."

"Lieutenant Walker, homicide.".

"Go ahead, Lester," Louise said, advising the call was live.

"Ron, I just—"

"I just got it off the wire. The captain called Miami. I'm on my way and I'll meet you there. We can use you. Get Gloria."

"Louise, call Gloria. Tell her. I'm on my way to pick her up."

"She's on the phone. She just heard the report on the scanner. She said she'll be ready. Pick her up."

Lester's Caddy barreled down Old Dixie Highway to Gloria's apartment. His foot pressed hard on the accelerator and wasn't coming off if he could help it. He knew all the cops around this area. Whenever they could, they picked his mind about his career in homicide in New York City—considered by many the greatest city. Miami was still developing, and even with the Silver Slipper and its infamous Palm Island resident didn't compare to the culture, the entertainment, Wall Street, *The Miracle on Thirty-Fourth Street*,[19] Macy's and the number of murders that happened each day. This time, the multiple murders were in Miami. Murders that would go down in the books as extraordinary. The '48 Caddy made it in record time with no red lights or red bubble lights swirling on cop cars to hinder his arrival. Gloria got in and they continued on US Highway One to Miami.

The security guard at Palm Oaks had a list of non-residents allowed entry because of the cordoned off areas by police barriers, patrol and unmarked cars, and ambulances that were of no use to the three dead inside the opulent home of Dr. and Mrs. Wanamaker. The dead were now the responsibility of the City of Miami Police

---

[19] Miracle on 34th Street is an American Christmas drama movie focusing on the effect of a department store Santa who claims to be the real Santa.

Detectives and the Miami Coroner. Just like any other crime scene in any other city or town in America, the reporters, often referred to as hound dogs, had used their police scanners to track news. They were on the scene as quickly as the police to report the big news of a triple homicide inside a gated community. A prominent wealthy doctor and his mistress killed in their home in sunny Miami, usually referred to as paradise, but not today. Today was a scene out of Hell.

Lester and Gloria saw Lieutenant Walker huddling with the Miami D.A. and detectives. A uniformed cop had Roslyn Wanamaker in custody.

"Where's this P.I. Caine Mrs. Wanamaker spoke of?" asked the D.A. Even with the gun she used lying on the dining room table, Roslyn wouldn't talk to anyone, just as Lorraine Vanderbilt had requested Lester. The difference was Lorraine didn't kill Desmond. Lester held a persuasive influence over people, women or men, a trait of a select few. They called it charisma or charm. He knew how to use it. His reputation always preceded him.

Lieutenant Walker spotted Lester, grabbing him by the arm as soon as they walked through the door. Walker had to move fast, although under pressure to make the introductions to the D.A. since Roslyn was keeping her yap shut.

"Listen, Caine and you too, Gloria," who was stuck firmly to Lester's side. "This was going to be a big hit for me and my department. What the fuck happened here? All this time, planning, and manpower down the toilet.

My brass will be all over me. This was supposed to be a Palm Beach collar. Now I've got to walk away from it."

"You'll get your turn, Ron. We can get this dame back in Palm Beach because that's where she first made contact about a murder for hire and she wanted to know how she could get a gun for protection."

"And I told you we have a fix on the perp, Thomas Fairchild. We can do it your way and get a warrant or we can bring him in our way," Gloria said.

"What are you talking about?" Ron questioned. At that moment, the D.A. joined the trio.

"I'm sorry, Bill. This is Private Investigator Lester Caine and his associate, Gloria Saville. This is William Short, Miami D.A."

"Your reputation precedes you, Mr. Caine. One of my detectives will be close by. Go do your magic, whatever it is. We have the smoking gun. We need a confession."

"Call me, Lester...Bill. I will help you bring her to justice. I'd like to walk the crime scene first. She's not going anywhere, and this is going to take us through the day and night."

"You're right. I just don't want her to fade away into some stupor, if you know what I mean. You must have seen that during your years on the force. You have until the coroner arrives and he will be here shortly."

"I'll do my best," Lester said, knowing the coroner would take at least an hour after he got here with three homicides.

The bloodied bodies were in three different areas of the house. The Miami Police had not had a gruesome scene like this since the days of big Al and his Chicago imports. It was a bloody mess.

Jean-Paul lay against the wall, his head slumped into his chest next to the slider door leading to the outside pool. A stray shot had shattered the glass. Blood soiled his shirt and pooled around him. The splatter of blood on the wall was like a wide brush stroke from an artist's abstract painting—Laurent's bloodied hand print stained the wall. This, detectives said, was him trying not to collapse and get out of the house.

"Who's gonna get the sand soldiers their patent leather boots now?" Gloria said.

"I guess we dodged that bullet and he didn't," Lester said, the twist of his lips the semblance of a smirk.

Millie Sparks lay naked with her head on the steps and one foot caught between the baluster railings, trying to escape Roslyn's wrath. Blood dripped along three steps before ending its trail. Roslyn's shot in Millie's left breast pierced her heart. Her adrenaline to escape so high she took a few steps before collapsing into the arms of the Grim Reaper.

Dr. Wayne Wanamaker never had time to get out of bed. Blood and gore splattered the headboard, lamp shade, night table, and carpet. His blood had soaked into the bedding. Roslyn must have shot the doctor four times from the shell casings that spewed from the semi-automatic—two in the chest, one in the eye entering his brain, and one in the groin. Lester's years as a lead homicide detective had taught him a lot about how to read a crime scene. This one was no different. The police had already bagged the colloquial *smoking gun*. He asked to see it, a Browning Hi-Powered 9mm with a ten-round capacity. His expert knowledge of weapons knew the power of this beast. A single round travels at 1,230 feet per second. Not one victim had a chance of escape. It's a wonder that Roslyn's firing wildly hit the doctor at all, since three bullets were embedded in the wall.

The damage caused by projectiles is a function of their kinetic energy, which is transferred to the victim on impact. As the bullet enters the body, it crushes and shreds tissue in its path. This creates a permanent cavity—the bullet hole.

In addition, the energy of the impact dissipates in a shock wave that radially flings surrounding tissue away from the path of the projectile, creating a cavity larger than the diameter of the bullet when it first entered the body.

Gloria, Lester, and the detective walked to where uniformed officers detained Roslyn. She sat on the couch with her hands cuffed behind her back, the usual police procedure with the perpetrator in custody.

Roslyn was a mess. Her blank stare compared to a dead fish. She had blood splatter on her face and dress.

"Uncuff her, please," Lester requested. An officer looked toward his boss, who observed from the doorway. He jerked his head.

"Roslyn, you know you're in deep shit here?" Lester said.

"It seems that way, doesn't it, Lester? I couldn't take it any longer. Wayne and Millie were together...here... in our bed."

"Roslyn, are you saying you killed your husband, Millie, and Jean-Paul?"

"Yes, Lester. I did it. They were having sex under my roof and in my bed. I was afraid for my life. He was going to have me killed. You know that. I told you. That's why I hired you. I was on edge. I couldn't sleep. Wayne saw I wasn't myself. He prescribed sleeping pills for me, but I couldn't take them. He was trying to drug me. I was going to be killed by him. I'm innocent. "

"What about Jean-Paul?"

"What the fuck about him? He was the hired gun, and Millie was his sister."

Lester turned to Gloria. Neither saw that coming and they couldn't hide their astonishment.

"She had to be in on it or know about it. Between the three of them, I was doomed. I feel sick. I'm going to throw-up."

"Someone get her something," Lester called to the medics.

Roslyn slumped, fainted. Gloria went to get a wet towel from the kitchen and held it on her forehead. The coroner saw what happened. He snapped an ammonia stick and placed it under Roslyn's nose, awakening her instantly.

"She'll be okay now," he said, walking back to continue his examination of the bodies.

"Roslyn, we can get you an attorney," Lester said. "You're going to need one. You'll be alright for now.

The police have to take you to the police station. You'll be put under arrest. We'll go with you and meet the attorney there. You've just confessed to killing three people. This is going to take time to sort through."

Gloria tried to comfort her. "Roslyn, these officers are going to escort you to the police station. Do you understand what is going to happen?" She continued as the officers again cuffed Roslyn's hands behind her back.

Lester asked the lead detective to use the phone. It hadn't been used in the commitment of a crime. A neighbor had called the police after hearing gunshots. He had to get Libby and H-2. After speaking with them, he dialed Louise. Lorraine had been calling non-stop along with Bert, the Palm Beach desk sergeant.

"Bert wants you to speak to Lorraine. Get her to back off going to the station day after day," Louise said. Lester finished his calls and turned to Gloria.

"What the fuck happened here? We've got to get our files together. We'll be dragged into this for sure. I reached Libby. They'll meet us. I spoke with Louise too. Lorraine is sniping at the Palm Beach Police, and the Palm Beach Police want me to get her to stop going to the station. Has Walker said anything to you about Lorraine showing up there?"

"No, not about Lorraine. But I told you, this dame was off the rails and she just caused one hell of a train wreck."

"Where is Jean-Paul's wife? Does anyone know?" Lester asked, raising his voice for everyone in the room to hear.

Heads turned with the quizzical look that resonated on everyone's faces...h*e has a wife*?

D.A. Bill Short turned to the lead detective. "You'd better get your ass on that now. Find out who and where she is."

CHAPTER 43

The Miami Tribune

PROMINENT VASCULAR SURGEON DEAD!

WIFE COMMITS TRIPLE MURDER!

Wayne Wanamaker, Millie Sparks and Jean-Paul Laurent, Victims

See coverage on Page 3 for Millie Sparks and Jean-Paul Laurent.

The tabloids had a field day. Newsstands hawked special editions of newspapers on street corners, the ink still wet. Grainy photographs of Roslyn led from her Miami home supplemented page 3 coverage.

A reporter for channel 23 delivered his report from Palm Oaks.

"I'm standing in front of the home of Dr. and Mrs. Wanamaker, the scene of a triple murder. A Miami prominent vascular surgeon, Dr. Wayne Wanamaker, gunned down along with two guests in his home. They have identified the other victims as Millie Sparks of Connecticut and Jean-Paul Laurent, a Miami resident. Police handcuffed Mrs. Wanamaker and are escorting her to the police squad car."

Covering the microphone, he turned to his cameraman. "Did you get a shot of the broad taken to the car?"

"Here comes the coroner. Ambulances line the drive. They're bringing the victims out, one gurney after the other. The procession looks like a parade of painted floats. Blood-stained sheets like a surreal painting cover the victims."

A gust of wind off the ocean fluttered the sheets.

"OH MY GOD! The sheet on the second gurney is loose. The coroner's aides are grabbing at it, but it's blowing in the stiff breeze like a sail."

Muffled words to the cameraman interrupted his narrative. "Zoom in on that. Get a closeup of the body. This is award-winning stuff!"

"Ladies and gentlemen, that's the naked body of a victim. It looks like a female," the excited announcer said. "What a horrific scene. Dr. Wanamaker, a respected surgeon, saved many lives during his career. He was a resident physician at Florida General, and a graduate of Johns Hopkins University-Baltimore. Miami will sorely miss his professional skills."

"Stay tuned to this station as we continue up to the minute coverage."

Libby and H-2 met with Roslyn every day within the guidelines of the jail's visiting hours, seven days a week, for attorneys and their clients. Libby planned to push for the M'Naghten rule, named for Daniel M'Naghten.[20] The M'Naghten case set a precedent of not guilty by insanity, and the basis for Roslyn's defense. Was Roslyn Wanamaker, the defendant, so deranged she did not know the nature or quality of her actions? Or, if she knew the nature and quality of her actions, was she so deranged that she did not know what she did was wrong?

The matron made consults difficult, particularly for women charged with murder and even more so for multiple murders. She caught wind of Libby's defense strategy. This incited her. She had a history of making defendant's attorney cool his heels. Many times, his wait could be two hours before he met with his client. By then, only a half hour consult was possible before the defendant had to return to her cell.

Libby and H-2 knew of the matron's stance and brought pizzas and beer for the guards. Scotch for the matron greased the wheel, and they had easy access.

Libby pushed for Roslyn's hearing before Judge Murdock's calendar, knowing of his sympathy for the

---

[20] The M'Naghten rule is named after Daniel M'Naghten, who in 1843, tried to kill England's prime minister, Sir Robert Peel. M'Naghten thought Peel wanted to kill him, so he tried to shoot Peel but shot and killed Peel's secretary, Edward Drummond. Medical experts testified M'Naghten was psychotic, and he was found not guilty by reason of insanity.

criminally insane. His brother was serving a life sentence in a psychiatric facility for the criminally insane after he murdered his wife and her lover.

Libby and H-2 successfully manipulated the pre-trial before Judge Murdock and the clerk set it on the court docket. They filed their "M'Naghten Rule, Notice of Insanity Defense," petitioning the court for psychiatric evaluation of Roslyn Wanamaker to prove she was mentally insane at the time she committed the three murders. H-2 cited *State vs. Pike (1869)*, where the court wrote, *"An accused is not criminally responsible if his unlawful act was the product of mental disease or mental defect."*

At the preliminary hearing, Judge Murdock granted Libby and H-2's petition. He denied bail. A court-appointed psychiatrist would evaluate Roslyn. In addition, the defendant's legal counsel would have a team of psychiatrists examine their client.

A panel of residents of Dade County registered voters representing the defendant's peers were assembled. Their selection by some unknown process sometimes resulted in *professional* jurors, as they were regularly called to serve. Defendant's lawyers and the District Attorney evaluated candidates through a process known as *voir dire* to determine the makeup of the jury—twelve citizens plus three alternatives—under the eyes of the Judge who would preside over the trial. This lengthy and contentious process required skill by both sides, prosecution and defense, to select an impartial jury.

The circus performers—reporters and cameramen— outside the courthouse and inside the lobby diminished in number during jury selection, appearing only as the attorneys or D.A. left the courthouse, hoping for a quote or names of jurors selected. The madness would increase in volume and frenzy when the trial began. Meanwhile, Roslyn awaited trial.

CHAPTER 44

1868 Wilshire Court

The Estate of Lorraine Vanderbilt.

L ester's Caddy zipped into the circular drive. He again marveled at this picturesque property with its magazine layout.

His Honor Judge Vanderbilt and Lorraine never brandished their wealth, but remembered their humble youth. They recognized the struggles of people in the same impoverished circumstances that had motivated them to succeed.

Not everyone possessed the tenacity required to accomplish such heights. A subconscious fear of success, which led to going through the motions, sabotaged many individuals' chances. That described Desmond's murderer, Thomas Fairchild. His parents' wealth provided a quality education and the backing to achieve whatever he set out to do. Instead, revenge and hubris trampled his heart. Every stomp drove another nail into his psyche, putting him on the road to Perdition.

"Good morning, Mr. Caine. Miss Lorraine is in her usual spot."

"Rosemary, please announce me. I don't want to catch her in a compromising—"

"Say no more, Mr. Caine." she interrupted. But she mumbled under her breath, "she probably would like you to compromise her."

"Lester, come here and don't be so shy. Hand me my robe if you'll be more comfortable." Shrugging into it and fluffing her hair, she said, "I know why you're here. And no, I will not stop going to the Palm Beach Police Station. Desmond was a dedicated judge, a good person, and a philanthropist. They owe him. They should spend every goddamn second on solving and capturing his killer. I will not stand for anything less. Or from you, like it or not."

Cleopatra, in all her glory, couldn't be more beautiful than Lorraine. Lester heard her words, but they failed in their effect. His libido wandered while his eyes ravished her body, still as lovely as her days as a performer.

"Lester, have you heard anything I said? You need a drink. Rosemary," she called.

"Lorraine, you know I'm devoted to solving Desmond's murder. I told you we have to get proof in order to prosecute the scumbag we think did it. But proof doesn't appear out of thin air. We know where he is and we have to follow rules so he doesn't skinny through a loophole. You know we have to have enough probable cause for a search warrant and enough evidence to charge him. Evidence leads to a conviction, not emotion."

"So, when are you getting this son-of-a-bitch?"

"I just told you. We are closing in on him. Gloria and I are doing everything we can, including crossing the line."

"Lester, relax. Take off your goddamn jacket and at least loosen your tie. Let's go for a swim," she teased.

"Lorraine..."

"C'mon, Lester. I feel like I'm the one serving time. I just thought we might have a little fun, maybe turn back the clock to our days in New York. You know, have a few laughs instead of hanging the crepe."

"Here's your drink, Mr. Caine."

"Rosemary, Mr. Caine will stay for lunch," she said, dropping her robe and testing the pool water, one stair step at a time.

"Yes, Miss Lorraine," Rosemary said, paying no attention to her antics.

CHAPTER 45

Clematis Street

Gloria entered Lester Caine Investigations.

"Hi, Gloria," said Louise. "He's in his office. Go ahead in. He won't mind."

"Gloria," Lester said in surprise. "I thought we were meeting later for dinner. Is everything okay?"

"Yes, of course. Can't we spend time together other than dinner and bed?"

"Well, okay. Did you have anything particular in mind?"

"Maybe."

"The zoo?"

"No."

"The beach?"

"No."

"The pool at my place? I'll have Louise postpone my appointments."

Gloria plopped onto Lester's lap. "Yes, have Louise rearrange your appointments and put me in for the entire day.... in ink."

Gloria's attitude puzzled Lester. He couldn't make heads or tails of her. Two failed marriages had shown him how fickle and unreliable women could be. His two ex-wives and Roslyn Wanamaker were examples.

"Lester. What a surprise. I didn't expect you. Did I call you?"

"No, Mom," he said after thinking a moment. "I wanted to stop by."

"Ahem!" Gloria cleared her throat.

"And who is this lovely young lady, Lester?"

"Mom, this is Gloria Saville. She's a private detective and an associate of mine."

"Welcome, my dear. Lester never brings a guest with him. I'm happy you've joined him. I'll put up some coffee. Sit, please."

"Let me help you, Mrs. Caine."

"Only if you call me Pamela."

"Of course, Pamela." She turned to Lester with a pleased smile.

"That's a lovely two-piece pantsuit you're wearing. Looks like Mother of the Bride Chiffon in pale sky blue," Pamela said.

"It is. How did you know?"

"Thirty years as a seamstress in the sweatshops in lower Manhattan."

Gloria turned to Lester with a quick wink.

"Did Lester ever tell you about Francis?" Pamela asked. "Let me show you some photos of all his performances. He was very talented, you know." Pamela led Gloria by the hand.

CHAPTER 46

Palm Beach Police Headquarters

L ester and Gloria swung by the Palm Beach Police Headquarters after leaving Pamela's. A new face greeted them, one they'd never seen before.

"Can I help you?" the desk sergeant asked.

"I'm Lester Caine and this is Gloria Saville." Both showed their identifications. "I guess Bert finally pulled the trigger in a manner of speaking."

"Well, let's hope not. He was under a lot of stress. I hope the salt air and being on his boat improves his outlook. Maybe he'll smile again before it's too late. I guess you want to see the 'Lu.' Sit tight. I'll buzz him."

"I'm glad you stopped in. We have some good news, thanks to you two," Walker said. "I may think about a new career as a P.I. when I retire. It appears it's been good to you."

"It has, but it has its own set of challenges, as you well know, wearing the badge and being on the job," Lester said.

"Well, this is what we have. We have positively identified Thomas Fairchild holed up at the Princess Ann Hotel and tracked his comings and goings."

"Good news, finally," Gloria said. "What's your next step? Remember what I told you about nabbing him your way or our way?"

"What Gloria's saying," Lester interjected, not willing to admit to any wrongdoing or what Walker would consider against the law.

"I know exactly what she's saying, Caine. I know what you both can do and how you do it. I cannot go that route. We want a solid conviction with no surprise endings that makes us run with our tails between our legs."

"Say no more. What's your plan?" Lester asked.

"Simple. We're getting a warrant and we're going in gang busters. I'm letting you know because you both deserve to be there."

"When?"

"Tomorrow at 0600 hours."

"No problem, Ron. Where do we rendezvous?" Lester asked.

"On the west side of the building. His room faces the rear. There is no way he will see us there. He usually leaves around 0800 hours. I'll have some gear for you both," Ron said.

"Good man, Ron."

"Remember that. Maybe you'll go easy with your invoice to the department."

Lester just smiled. "If there's nothing else, we'll see you at 0600 hours."

"One more thing. US intelligence found Jean-Paul's wife hiding out in Israel. And guess what? She's an Israeli national. The Department of State can't extradite her."

The Morning of the Takedown

0530

Lester drove his Caddy slowly on the quiet streets, empty at that hour. He parked down the street from the Princess Ann Hotel. Walker's men were gearing up when they arrived. Lester hadn't been on one of these door busters in a while.

He knew how intense the adrenaline became. Each tick of his watch kicked his senses into overdrive. Walker handed vests to Lester and Gloria with POLICE printed in bold letters, front and back.

"You know the drill. First man up, the enforcer; second, my sergeant with the warrant; breachers, me, my men; then you two. Got it?"

"Ten-four, Lieutenant. We're ready," said Lester.

They lined up in a single file with one hand on the shoulder of the man in front of them. Their other hand held their weapon. Their step was a soft tap, giving an eerie appearance of a chorus line, but so little sound for so many men, heavily suited and armed.

Lieutenant Walker entered the hotel door first, going directly to the desk clerk. Walker's POLICE vest and drawn weapon visibly terrified her. Walker held his finger to his lips in the quiet sign. Fright made her step back from the desk.

He whispered, "Do not pick up that phone," and took the receiver off the cradle. "Step out from behind the desk, sit over there, and don't say a word," pointing to the plush lobby chair. "If you do as I say, you should be safe." He signaled for one of his men to stand by her.

The policemen climbed softly up the stairwell, keeping their cadence. Walker joined them, stepping past each man, tapping him as he passed. No one spoke, using only hand signals. When they reached the door to the hallway leading to Fairchild's room, they pressed close to the wall. Once in place, each man in succession nodded they were ready, and waited for Walker's last nod.

The Enforcer's fist hit the door. BANG! ... BANG! ... BANG, followed by the Sergeant's shout, "Palm Beach Police, Warrant. Open the door." No answer within what Lester used to call his three-second rule 'offer.' One Mississippi, two Mississippi, three Mississippi immediately followed by the Enforcer swinging the fifty-pound steel ram rod to bust through the door, the oldest siege weapon in use, dating back to the ninth century[21].

The door splintered like a tree felled by a lumberjack's axe, followed by the entourage stomping and yelling. Police used this tactic to confuse and disorient the alleged criminal about to go down. Occupants of rooms up and down the hallway opened their doors, curious to see what the chaos was about.

Thomas Fairchild awakened to the thunderous sound of feet pounding and voices yelling. He jumped from the bed, shocked at the arsenal of weapons pointing at him. Momentarily frozen, he stood there blinking, his eyes still blurred with sleep. He raised his arm, holding the gun he slept with, a deadly reflex with no conscious thought.

Shots rang out, penetrating his body. Police riddled his body with bullets, ushering Thomas Fairchild to his grave.

Gloria bowed her head, taking in a deep breath before letting out a sigh. She imagined the agony his mother would face hearing of her son's death and identifying his body.

---

[21] In the ninth century the Assyrians used it to break through gatehouses and castle walls. *'If it was good enough for them, it's good enough for us,* was the police motto.'

"Gloria, I have to go. I have to get to Lorraine before Fairchild's death hits the wire. She has to hear from me that Desmond got justice," Lester said.

Channel 23 set up outside the hotel, their newsman suitably somber.

"I'm standing outside the Princess Ann Hotel, the scene of a predawn raid by the Palm Beach Police."

"Police gunned down Thomas Fairchild in what hotel guests described as a bloody massacre. In a predawn raid, a squad of Palm Beach Police invaded the Princess Ann Hotel, storming up the stairs and into Mr. Fairchild's room, ending his life in a hail of bullets."

"Lead Detective Walker asserted they had probable cause and an arrest warrant. Thomas Fairchild allegedly did not respond to Police requests to surrender. Police broke down the door and entered his room. Mr. Fairchild attempted to fire his weapon at the Police."

"Mr. Fairchild was the son of Cynthia Fairchild. You may recall the sensational trial years ago in Miami. Mrs. Fairchild, nee Cynthia Beall, and her lover, a priest in the Miami diocese, were charged with murdering Mrs. Beall's husband. Desmond Vanderbilt was the attorney of record for the defense and won an acquittal for Mr. and Mrs. Fairchild. Police speculate that Thomas Fairchild killed Desmond Vanderbilt to avenge what he perceived as a miscarriage of justice in his father's death."

As horrific as the newspaper and television reports were, this event would impact Cynthia Fairchild, like the aftershock of an earthquake. Her son murdered

Desmond Vanderbilt, the lawyer who got her and her husband acquitted of the murder of Thomas's father. Vanderbilt had helped them realize the life they wanted together and had given them the opportunity for wealth.

"The Desmond Vanderbilt case has come full circle," Gloria said, sipping her vodka martini. "Do you think his mother and stepfather will ever think their love was worth the lives it cost? This has to be the hand of payback."

"It's called Karma," Lester said.

CHAPTER 47

L ibby St. James pushed the door open to *Lester Caine Investigations*, and marched past Louise, her gaze determined, without uttering a word.

Louise jumped to her feet, but Libby held her hand up without skipping a step.

"Don't bother, Louise." She opened the door to Lester's office.

"Libby?" Lester questioned, standing. "To what do I owe a visit from one of Vanderbilt, Harper & St James's finest?" He turned to Louise, standing ready at the door. "It's alright, Louise. Close the door."

"Don't play games with me, Lester. I know you have the envelope. H-2 and I need it. We can work on this together. We're prepared to include you... and Lorraine too."

I would like to thank you for choosing my novels. This is an important part of my journey as an author, having you as the reader.

All online book sellers use reviews in their algorithms for book placement.

Your opinion matters to me. One way to enrich readership is with your review.

I would appreciate if you took a moment to leave a review so others can receive the same benefits you have–being taken away to another time and place.

Thank you. I hope you enjoy many of my writings.

Amazon.

Barnes & Noble

Walmart

Books-a-Million

Kindle

Nook

Audible.

Sincerely,

fred berri

Don't forget to subscribe for advanced special offers, bonus content, updates from the author and info on new releases.

Go to:

fredberri.com

REFERENCES

Jim Beam-Whiskey distillers established 1795 as Old Tub Bourbon by Jacob Beam.

Brooks Brothers-The oldest clothing retailer in the U.S. headquartered in NYC founded in 1818 by Henry Sands Brooks opened as H&DH Brooks & Co. His four sons inherited the business and, in 1850, renamed the company "Brooks Brothers." They have outfitted almost every President of the United States.

Allen Edmonds-An American upscale shoe company established in 1922. Their shoes are worn by U.S. Naval officers and Presidents of the U.S.

Taylor of Old Bond Street- One of the oldest and most respected barbershops in the world. The company formed in 1854 by Jeremiah Taylor on London's fashionable Bond Street, also supplying high end men's grooming products throughout the world.

Jack Daniels Tennessee Whiskey- Jasper Newton Daniel, commonly known as Jack, introduces the world to his signature charcoal-mellowed Tennessee Whiskey-Old No. 7 in 1864. Jack Daniels' Whiskey is one of the most popular Whiskeys to this day.

Burdine Department Stores-started in 1897 and grew into a multi-department store chain in Florida known for its Florida culture in the design and décor of its stores.

Paul Gauguin-1848-1903 French Artist.

Pierre-Auguste Renoir -1841-1919. French artist.

AP-Associated Press is an independent global news organization dedicated to factual reporting. Founded in 1846.

The Hialeah Park Race Track is one of the oldest existing recreational facilities in southern Florida. Originally opened in 1922 by aviation pioneer Glenn Curtiss and his partner, Missouri cattleman James H. Bright, as part of their development of the town of Hialeah, Florida.

Flora and Fauna-Flora refers to all plant life & Fauna is the population of animal life in a particular region or time.

Across the Board Racing Bet-A bet on a horse to win, place, and show. If the horse wins, the bettor collects three ways; if second, two ways (place, show); and if third, one way, losing the win and place bets. It's actually three bets.

Mudder-is a horse that races well on a wet track. An example of a Mudder is the horse that wins several races on a rainy day.

Lauren Bacall-an American Icon Actress.

Frank Sinatra-Frank Sinatra was an American singer and actor who is generally perceived as one of the greatest musical artists of the 20th century.

Paramount Theater- was a 3,664-seat theater at 43rd Street and Broadway in Times Square, New York City, 1926,

A&P Supermarket-The Great Atlantic & Pacific Tea Company, better known as **A&P**, was an American chain of grocery stores that operated from 1859 to 2015. From 1915 through 1975, A&P was the largest grocery retailer in the United States & Canada and until 1965, the largest U.S. retailer of any kind.

Colony Hotel-A small luxury boutique hotel on Palm Beach, Florida

Testa's Restaurant-An iconic restaurant 1921-2017, Royal Poinciana Way, Palm Beach, Florida

Arthur Murray Dance Studios-Established 1925 to give all different dance lessons.

Dilly Dally Deli Catering-Fictitious name by author, fred berri.

Saxony Hotel-The Saxony Hotel was one of the first luxury hotels in Miami.

Miaflo Assembly Co.-Fictitious company created by author, fred berri. Miaflo is an acronym for Miami Florida.

Fact: **Naval Amphibious Training Base** 128 miles north in Ft. Pierce, trained 40,000 troops for the invasion of Normandy was indeed true.

Silver Slipper-Fictitious restaurant by author, fred berri.

Nedick's-was an American chain of fast-food restaurants that originated in New York City in 1913. The name of the chain was formed from the last names of Robert T. Neely and Orville A. Dickinson.

Chuck Full of Nuts-Chock full o'Nuts is an American brand of coffee that originated from a chain of New York City coffee shops. Its unusual name derives

from the 18 nut shops that founder William Black (c. 1902 – 1983) established under that banner in the city beginning in 1926. When the Great Depression struck, he converted them to lunch counters, serving a cup of coffee and a sandwich for five cents.

Jesus H Christ-an expletive interjection that refers to the Christian religious figure of Jesus Christ. It is typically uttered in anger, surprise, or frustration.

Florida State Supreme Court-State supreme courts are completely distinct from any United States federal courts located within the geographical boundaries of a state's territory, or the federal-level Supreme Court. The exact duties and powers of the state supreme courts are established by state constitutions and state law.

Machine Gun Kelly-An American Gangster from Memphis, Tennessee who used a Thompson submachine gun kidnapping oil tycoon, Charles F. Urschel.

Millard Caldwell-Florida Governor 1945-1949

Midnight Train& Lola's Jazz Club-Fictitious Jazz club and ensemble with fictitious musicians by author, fred berri.

No shit Sherlock-To express the view that someone is stating something that is completely obvious as the fictional character of Detective Sherlock Holmes.

The Life of Rile- The term *living the life of Riley* is an American phrase, it first appeared in the early 1900s. It means living the easy life, an existence marked by luxury and a carefree attitude.

Princess Ann Hotel-Fictitious named hotel by author.

10328 W. Royal Palm Way, Miami, Florida—Palm Oaks-The fictitious address of Dr. Wayne and Roslyn Wanamaker.

French Besson Brevete Trumpet- In 1837. Gustave Auguste Besson manufactured brass instruments in Paris.

Billy Holiday-**Billie Holiday** (born **Eleanora Fagan)**; American jazz and swing music singer Nicknamed **"Lady Day."**

Shinola is a defunct American brand of shoe polish. The colloquialism, not knowing shit from Shinola was used where the shoe polish color brown was a reminder of the color of *shit* not being able to tell one from the other. It's intended meaning is you don't know what you're talking about.

ACKNOWLEDGEMENTS

Publisher- frederic dalberri

Editor ––– jc konitz

Cover ––– Judith San Nicolas

(judithsdesign.com)

Interior Formatting---Shahbaz Awan

SPECIAL THANKS TO...

My wife Louisa and my Physical Therapist Anne Jackson, helping name protagonist, Lester Caine.

Steve Pierangeli for his authentic life's experience supplying Patent Leather boots to foreign Eastern soldiers to wear in the desert.

'Chip' Marker for sharing his authentic story of his attorney father caring for widows who lost all their money in the depression–continuing to pay them without them knowing their loss.

Sonny Abbott-My great friend, Millicent's father. RIP.

All Books by fred berri

Available:

Amazon, Barnes & Noble, Kindle, Nook, Audible, Walmart, Books-a-Million

&

All online book outlets and fredberri.com

* * *

Cousins' Bad Blood

Cousins' Bad Blood-The Take Over

Murder on Contadora Island

* * *

Books featuring Homicide Detective Johnny Vero

Ten Cents a Dance

Bullets Before Dawn-Murder in Chinatown

Sabre Blue Society

* * *

Books featuring Adventures of Carmelo™

Swim Survival Lessons–The Dentist–The Eye Doctor–

Going to the Hospital–Jiu Jitsu

Coloring Book

The Adventures of Carmelo™ is a series of children's learning stories. These stories help children understand new adventures, teaching respect, listening, following instructions, to be brave, and that it's okay to be scared when facing a new adventure.

Coming Soon; Lester Caine-Private Eye--Pigpen Cipher

Adventures of Carmelo—A New Puppy

About the Author

    Mr. Berri graduated Columbia State University with a business degree. He volunteered teaching Junior Achievement in the Florida school district and led a volunteer reading program for grades K-3. He has done public speaking and appeared in TV commercials and voice overs. Berri has written numerous murder mysteries and children's books which can be found:

website: **fredberri.com**

Amazon

Barnes & Noble

Walmart

Books-a-Million

Kindle

Nook

Audible

And all Online book sellers.

5 Star Award-winning Author

fredberri.com

Printed in the USA
CPSIA information can be obtained
at www.ICGtesting.com
LVHW090251060124
768161LV00011B/253